SONGBIRDS

Piper Huguley Deborah Fletcher Mello Iris Bolling

♪ ♪

♪

Printed in the United States of America

ISBN: 978-0-9913426-9-3

Library of Congress Control Number: 2017907839

This is a work of fiction. Names, characters, places and incidents are with the product of the author's imagination or are used fictitiously, and any resemblance to actual persons, living or dead, business establishments, events, locales is entirely coincidental.

SIRI AUSTIN ENTERTAINMENT LLC
RICHMOND, VIRGINIA
www.siriaustin.com
www.irisbolling.net

To all of the Songbirds who paved the way:
May your song echo in our hearts forever.

Sparrow's Song

by

Piper Huguley

CHAPTER ONE

Before she died, Sparrow St. Clair had one request. She reached her arms out, toward the ones she loved best in this world, in the place she loved best, the home her beloved Chuck had built with his own hands. She extended an arm to her daughter Lark whose brow was all scrunched up with worry. The other arm went to her grandbaby Dove, face smooth and unlined, unafraid of the future, but full of the blood surging beneath her smooth brown skin. The blood would tell, as they said. Her blood would carry the hope and promise forward. Her blood would finish the work she had failed to complete.

So, she wasn't sorrowful at the prospect of this dying. She was just tired, eager to cast off this shell that had failed her by falling and getting sick. It was time, time for her to soar on her bird's wings to Jesus.

"I want you, both of you, to sing my song for me. Sing it to me."

Lark's pretty face scrunched up even more. "This isn't a time for singing, Mama. You need rest and quiet."

"The white people in the neighborhood will hear," Dove whispered, as if she was ashamed of what she sounded like.

The blood surged within Sparrow. It was like the moon overhead tugged on her, like the cord pulled out of that old doll she had given to Carole once. She sat straight up in the hospital bed they had rented for her, moving quick like she hadn't in years. "Where's Carole?"

Lark laid an arm on her. "She's coming, Mama. She'll be here soon."

"I've got to say..." She grasped at their hands, one on each side.

"Rest, Grandmama. You got to rest," Dove pleaded.

Only the sheen of tears in her grandbaby's eyes made her hesitate and stilled her tongue on what she wanted to say.

"I will." She grasped the girl's hands. "But I don't ever, *ever* want you to be ashamed of your voice. Not anywhere. I don't care who hears you. This world needs to hear what we know. What *we* been knowing."

The strength in Sparrow ebbed as she laid back against the pillows Lark had hurriedly rearranged for her comfort.

It did feel good to get back on the pillows. But she wasn't going to have no shame. Shame was a stilling and powerful force. Shame is what kept Sparrow from fulfilling her dreams. She wouldn't let it get her grandbaby. It might be too late for Lark, but not Dove.

She gripped their hands in hers, Lark on her left, Dove on the right. "Sing the song. I want to hear it. Call it my last request if you have to, but sing my song. *Right now.*"

She focused on each one of their faces and noticed the tears coming down. Well, that was to be expected under the circumstances, she guessed. She loved them and they loved her too. It was nice to know that before she went on to her heavenly kingdom. Sparrow only hoped she could hold on long enough to see Carole and say goodbye. After all, Carole was her first daughter. The first one she let into her heart. If it weren't for Carole, she wouldn't have made the room to love her man. Others called him JC, but she called him Chuck, a name she had given him herself that rhymed with what they liked to do best. If it hadn't been for her him, she wouldn't have these two loves right here who were taking in deep cleansing breaths to start singing her song in unison.

Their beautiful voices, strong and pure, floated over her. Oh, what would she give to be able to join in with them. But she had done all the singing she was going to do. She felt her hearts grasping her hands back and she shut her eyes, just to savor the beauty in the voices of her songbirds. Yes, Dove was doing as she was supposed to do. She was singing without shame, the only way to sing a song.

Listening, relaxing her body, Sparrow's mind returned to 1968. The song from her loved ones took her heart back to that hot Georgia summer when she first met Carole, and fell in love with Chuck. It was good to visit when her life began, now that it was ending.

CHAPTER TWO

The morning after her high school graduation, Sparrow Jones tried to pull the covers back over her pseudo afro and get some rest. Her mother would not let her. Sparrow knew she was taking a chance in defying Faitha Jones when she heard her calling. Her defiance drew her mother to her room to pull the covers down from her and to turn on the bright light.

"Get up, Sparrow. *Now.*"

Her mother's deep voice, colored by not having coffee before she rode two public buses deep into the city to clean houses for the white folks, showed that she was not having this particular brand of laziness.

Sparrow sat up in her pink nightdress and blinked, eyes hurting from adjusting to the light in her room.

Sparrow's eyes focused to see her mother's arms folded showing her displeasure at having to take this moment from her coffee.

"Yes, Mama?"

"Did you make up your mind?"

"About?"

"Girl, you know what I said to you. They gave you that degree. Use your head. Are you coming with me or you going down to the church for your job?"

"Mama, I told you about going to school."

"And I said to you, there's no money or time for that. You done with school. Got your high school diploma. Time to be a grown-up. You need to be helping around here with your brothers and sisters or you can put on this here dress and come with me."

Her mother clutched a gray maid's uniform in her hand.

"Don't have the right shoes."

"We can buy some."

"That looks too big for me."

"So, we will pin it up. It won't make no never mind when you get on your apron no way. What you going to do, Sparrow?"

"I would rather die than put that thing on."

Sparrow didn't mean her words to come out so disrespectfully. Still, the look of horror on her mother's face showed that's how she took it.

"So, you so grown now, that it? Got your diploma and you so full of yourself? You think I wouldn't have rather died too? 'Specially since that's how you came about, because I put on this ugly thing? No, I had to put it on so you could eat and your brothers and sisters could too. And you so grown you got the nerve to tell me all about what you are going to do."

"Mama...."

Her mother turned from her. "No, Sparrow. You go on down to the church. 'Cause that's clearly what you are needing. Reverend be glad to have you down there to run the summer program. Enjoy yourself. I'ma see you in the fall with this uniform on. Matter of fact, I'ma order your shoes, that's how I know."

Her mother stomped down the steps in her heavy, thick-soled practical shoes that would take a long, long time to wear out. Shoes that would take rain, walking, spills, and harsh treatment. Wasn't nothing destroying them shoes.

Sparrow wanted no parts of it. She hopped out of bed and stood, wishing her attempts to get an afro had worked. They hadn't. She looked like a toasty Mia Farrow instead. The black hairs on her head laid down in pixie cut rather than stand up in defiance as a crown and sign of Black power cause of the white in her. She hated the white in her. Ever since that terrible November day when they killed John Kennedy and another day of crushed hopes when they killed Bobby Kennedy, she knew she would only embrace the Black parts of her. No matter what people said, she would embrace the Blackness. It was safer that way.

She pulled out a dress that she wore in the spring when she was working for the Kennedy campaign in Georgia. It was gray and boring. She pulled the pinned Bobby Kennedy sash off the dress and pressed the dress down with her hands. It would do; she looked all-boring--like a church worker should. And she could move well in the dress, in case she had to chase after any kids she would have to watch for the summer program.

She picked up a brush and brushed her hair down while looking woefully at the afro pick she had bought, lying on her white-painted dresser in anticipation of the fro that would not exist.

It was time to start the rest of her life as a church worker, which was way better than becoming her mother. Although her dreams of singing for a Kennedy president were gone forever because of a couple of foolish assassins, so were her dreams of singing for powerful white men. It was better to have her own dreams. She would show her mother. Fall would bring a different Sparrow for sure.

It was never an easy task to get her two brothers and two sisters out of the house all together. Those children were noisy and a pain. But she didn't put up with their foolishness. And now that she was going to work at the church in Mrs. Lincoln's stead, she decided she would get her sisters, Beatrix and Candace lined up. She knew that her sisters thought she was bossy, but if they wanted their cut of her now higher salary of $500, they would be there for her.

Besides, her extremely good organizing skills were the reason the Reverend knew she could handle a job like running the summer camp program at Second Missionary Baptist Church. She nearly had Ronald and Donald, her eight-year-old twin brothers, by the tips of their dirty brown ears guiding them the three blocks that it took to get to the church building. The church was built in the aftermath of the Civil War by ~~the~~ recently freed slaves who wanted to worship God in gratitude that Emancipation had finally come. It was a big imposing brown building, but every time Sparrow stepped into it, she never forgot that first group of five couples who believed in their future enough to build such a structure to show God's glory. So, she knew that she could do something to get the church's children to learn and have fun over the next ten weeks.

"Morning, Sister Sparrow. So good to see you here ready to take charge."

"Good morning, Reverend. We are happy to help you," Sparrow said.

Sparrow used the rest of the morning with her sisters to plan the activities, set the camp's theme to honor a figure of Black history every week, and bake some snacks in the kitchen. Her sisters proved to be extremely useful in getting her brothers to behave. She set Bea to mind Ronald and Candace minded Donald. Yes, they were well worth the $50 bucks each that she would be paying them. Then, her mother would get a portion to help with the bills and the groceries. She might have enough left for a term for music school in the fall. She would figure out the rest for winter when it came to it. She couldn't lose it. God would help her find a way to her lifelong dream of singing for the President. It wouldn't be John or Robert Kennedy, but maybe it might be their little brother Ted.

When it was time for lunch, it was time to start the paperwork for the camp. Mrs. Lincoln, the woman who she was taking over for, would come to review how things were run with her. So they ate the peanut butter sandwiches and mushy apples the church provided along with two stale sugar cookies each and she sent her sisters and brothers home with stern warnings not to act up or out.

Rose Lincoln came in with a carriage and dressed in a flower print maternity dress. She was due to have her baby at any time and Sparrow was taking over for her this summer. Sparrow was a little fearful of Mrs. Lincoln because she was a teacher during the regular school year. But as a high school graduate, she was an adult just like Mrs. Lincoln. Funny how time changed things. "Call me Rose," she said when they sat down to determine Sparrow's job to check in the children and to keep order in the school.

"You can do this. I will come as I can, but I know I will be distracted for a time in a few weeks." Mrs. Lincoln stood there, then opened her pocketbook.

"I'm proud of you, Sparrow. I bought you something for your graduation."

She drew forward a small box and handed it to her. "Go on, open it."

"Right now?"

"Of course now."

She opened the paper carefully saving it and Mrs. Lincoln laughed. "Rip it off. What are you saving it for?"

Sparrow stopped. Mrs. Lincoln was right. She ripped into the striped paper and a Timex box emerged. "A watch. A bracelet watch. Thank you very much."

"You're welcome. It will be very important for you to keep time in your new job. You've got to be a role model for these children. One hundred children will be a lot. But I know you can do it, Sparrow."

They walked out to Mrs. Lincoln's car. She offered Sparrow a ride, but Sparrow turned her down. "I'll walk. Thank you."

Would she have come across Carole if she had decided to take a ride in Mrs. Lincoln's blue Mustang that day? What if she decided she was worth taking a spin in that cute teacher's car? But something, a word from up on high made her walk home that hot June day.

Part of her decision involved walking through the neighborhoods and waving hello to a number of the children she knew would come to the summer camp. Sparrow would bring them all together for the special children's service and pageant that took place right before Labor Day. Hers would be a little different than Mrs. Lincoln same old Bible stories. Nothing against them, but she was determined to show the strength and beauty of the people by having the children present something a bit different that would hopefully build pride and lift their spirits.

While she was thinking of the plot, and which soul songs the children would sing, she saw a beautiful child sitting on the edge of a lawn, wearing a sunny yellow dress. The child's dress was sunny, but she herself was not. And her hair was a mess.

"Hello." She waved to the child.

The small girl looked a little alarmed, but she said nothing. "Are you playing outside today? Jacks?"

The little girl indeed had ten multicolored metal jacks laying on the ground before her. "Where is your ball?"

Why didn't this child talk? Maybe she was shy. "Do you want to play? I'll beat you."

A smile came onto her pretty features and she shook her head. "Oh, I won't? Let's see then."

Sparrow could be competitive, but she was intrigued by the pretty girl. They played jacks in silence and the girl was right. She did win. But she didn't declare her groupings as someone was supposed to do before they played jacks. She held up fingers and expected Sparrow to interpret. So Sparrow spoke for her.

When they were done, Sparrow reached out to smooth the plaits of the child and asked the girl, "Where is your mother, honey?"

A look of horror crossed the child's face and she jumped up and ran into the Claiborne house. Sparrow stood on the sidewalk, not sure of what to do. Did the child run because she forgot her mother in the house? She was tempted to follow and see where the girl was going. Still, why was her hair so sloppy?

The child was a mystery for sure. Unfortunately, she had to get home and get dinner started before her own mother got home. She had done enough to displease her today. It wouldn't do any good to anger her any more than she already had.

CHAPTER THREE

The next day was Saturday, which meant that her mother was usually around. Faitha refused to work on the weekend. She was such a good maid that the white folks let her have off, even though other maids worked at least until two p.m. Sparrow never failed to be embarrassed by that allowance, because it meant that she was there to boss them around and force them to clean the house. It was the one day of the week when Sparrow aligned with her siblings since she had a completely different way of looking at the world than her mother did.

This Saturday though, was different. She worried about the little girl with the unkempt hair. What was she doing outside all by herself today? Did she have enough to eat? Maybe if she went to help her with her braids, the little girl would feel more comfortable and tell her about herself. Was she deaf and dumb? She didn't pull or tug at her ears. The thought of the little girl's liquid brown eyes tugged at something inside of her all morning.

Faitha was especially relentless. "I want that toilet to shine," she yelled at Sparrow standing over her. "Scrub hard at them spots."

When her mother walked away, Sparrow rolled her eyes, her sighs filling the bathroom. Scrubbing extra hard at them spots since that was the only way she could get back at her mother. Her mother's outbursts rained down on her only because she had her high school diploma. Faitha didn't. More likely than not, she would have to hear the narrative of her mother's life. Again.

"I only got eight grades. Back in them days, they would throw you out in the streets to work when you were 13. I learned how to do for myself when I was only Candace's age, just a few years older than the twins. Had to get up to get on the bus every day at 5 a.m. to work at cleaning white folks' houses. Brought my pay envelope home to my Daddy too. Until I had to leave."

Usually, this was the part of her mother's story when she would come and check on what Sparrow was doing. She would yell at her to move faster, scrub harder... something. Sparrow knew her birth was part of the leave taking. Her existence was the reason why there was a split between Faitha and Daddy Curtis. Something had happened to Faitha in one of those houses on the other side of Atlanta. Something horrible. Something that meant this was why Sparrow was here, cleaning toilets.

The tale usually gave her a sick feeling in the pit of her stomach, like she herself was on the edge of a cliff about to fall over. Never did she think of going on that side of Atlanta to look for herself, to see where she came from, to see who she came from. She hated all of it.

Today though, she didn't mind the cleaning chore as much. It gave her time to think about the little girl and to develop a plan after lunch to help the girl.

"What's wrong with you today?" Faitha came to inspect her cleaning work.

"I'm fine, Mama."

"You seem like you up to something."

"I went to the church. Got my job. What else, Mama?" Sparrow stood and pulled the rubber gloves off her hands with a thwack and tossed them into the sink to clean them and dry them.

Faitha gave her a look up and down her body. "You bringing one of them boys around?"

"I'm not interested in any of that."

"Yet."

"I don't know how I can be. You always got your eye on me."

Faitha stood a little closer to her. "Yes. My eye is on the Sparrow."

"Mama. Really."

Her mother gave a laugh. "You was primed for that. Take it like a woman. It's my job to have my eye on you, as you say."

"I'm grown now."

"Well good. The good way you cleaned that toilet got me thinking you ready to join me on the bus."

A shudder went through her. "I'm going to go out after we done cleaning and I've finished lunch."

"Going shopping?"

"No, ma'am. I just want to make sure all is ready for the camp."

"You a good girl, Sparrow. You need to study on keeping it that way. Don't end up like me."

"I'm doing all I can."

"Yeah. I can tell."

There was a fine sheen of tears on her mother's eyes. Sparrow had wounded her once more. Seemed like she could never stop hurting her mother. Her very presence hurt her. One day, she would have enough to leave this house behind her for good. But since she wanted to go to music school, that day seemed like it would never come. So, she would take the pain.

♩♩♩

After she fixed a stack of bologna sandwiches, cheese curls, cut up some apples and poured milk, Sparrow made sure to scatter her brothers and sisters for the day. Bea and Candy were going to use their hard-earned money to go to the hair salon to keep their beehive hairdos controlled. Sparrow shook her head. That was the entire point behind her pseudo Afro. No more beauty salon taking all day and putting smelly goopy stuff on her. She would go to the barber shop.

Only her plan didn't work. Her hair laid down in supplication, instead of puffing up in defiance. The barber, when he cut it, tried to reassure her that it would as it grew, but she didn't believe it.

Her sisters, looking lovely with their dark brown skins and proud walks, looked quite chummy going down the street to the bus stop. She hoped that they weren't looking to duplicate the life their mother had. Still if it weren't for her, they wouldn't have an ounce of determination to do anything. She couldn't worry about them now.

Her brothers ran outside, front door slamming, obviously trying to get away from their house full of women. Faitha yelled out, "Stop slamming my door!"

They were way too far to hear her anyway. Her brothers wouldn't be back until dinner time and near sundown.

The house was quiet, with Faitha in her perch in the living room, Otis Redding playing low, television playing. Her mother loved to watch the afternoon movies. Sparrow was usually horrified with her viewing choice, and how she loved to watch those movies on their black and white television of white folks falling in love.

She put on a white triangle mini dress today and brushed her black hair down on her head. Slipping on some white flats, she prepared to exit. Her mother's voice from the parlor rose above Otis's wailing about the dock he was sitting on near his bay. . "Leaving now?"

"Yes, Mama."

"You look nice. You can bring him here to the house to meet me you know."

"I'm not going out to meet some man."

"Hmmmm Hmmm." Faitha hummed and returned to watching *Stella Dallas.*

She had put a small brush in her purse with some barrettes, yarn ties and rubber bands of various sizes. Their jar of blue Afro Sheen grease was too large, so she put some into some aluminum foil and twisted it around to secure it, willing it not to melt in her purse. She didn't want to reach down into her purse and see a big grease spot, oozing of blue goo.

It took her about ten minutes to get to the Claiborne house. As Sparrow approached she found the little girl sitting on the front porch

Sparrow waved as she came closer to her. "Good morning. I brought some things to make your hair look nice. Would you like for me to help you?"

The girl's lovely eyes lit up and Sparrow sat down on the steps. She gestured for the small girl to ease into the time old position between her knees.

"I understand what it's like to want to look pretty. I wanted to look pretty, too. That's why I got all my hair cut off. Instead of a power 'fro though, I look like some white woman in a movie that's coming out. It will grow back out though. Then I'ma look righteous, like Angela Davis. You are a pretty young lady. About the age of my bad brothers. They are twins and I tell you... they are something. I gotta take care of them 'cause my Mama say so." She paused a moment, then asked, "Where's your mama?"

She knew the girl heard her because she stood up. When she turned and faced her, tears were running down her pretty brown face. Sparrow wanted to hug the girl, hold her close, but she didn't want to frighten the child.

"It's ok. I'm sorry. I won't hurt you. Let's finish making you look pretty. Come on now."

The girl looked like she wanted to run off again, but she knew that her hair wasn't finished yet and still was wiry all over her head.

Sparrow opened her white patent leather pocketbook. "Look what's in here. You can pick the ones that will make you look pretty. Maybe you will come to church with me tomorrow morning. Or the camp. I have a camp at our church about a five-minute walk from here. You can come and play with some other girls. We put on a music program."

Maybe her talking was making the child nervous. Although...she seemed to like Sparrow's pocketbook. She pulled the yarn ties and barrettes out and started selecting some.

Whew.

Sparrow thought to lift her voice in song. Her voice grew and lifted to the heavens as she sang the regular cycle of gospel songs and some patriotic songs, all of the songs that she was going to use in the program at the end of the summer term. Just as she clasped the last braid of hair on top of the girl's head after brushing it thoroughly, she was surprised to hear doors slamming inside the Claiborne house.

The little girl jumped up and huddled close to Sparrow. Naturally, she put her arms around the child to protect her. Who was this precious girl living with?

A man came to the door. He wore a pants and a sleeveless tee shirt that made his arms bulge out in a way that Sparrow hadn't seen up close before. They were truly remarkable.

"What's all of this singing going on out here? Who are you? Get your hands off my child!"

He stepped out closer to her reaching to retrieve the child from her, but Sparrow wouldn't let him. "She's frightened of you."

"Carole, baby, come here. You fine. Who is this lady?"

Sparrow stood, barrettes and yarn ties tumbling from her lap. "I'm Sparrow Jones. I'm in charge of the summer program at Second Missionary Baptist church down the street."

"Did you say your name was Sparrow?"

Ugh. She got this a lot. She stuck her chin out. "I did."

"Why in the hell did your Mama name you that? Ain't nothing spare about you."

"She called me that because she didn't want to call me Sorrow. That was supposed to be my real name. She named me something close."

The man ran a hand over his nappy head and seemed to realize that he looked less than presentable. "Carole is my daughter."

"She needed her hair braided. So I did it." Sparrow snapped the last barrette on Miss Carole's head and the girl ran into the house to look at a mirror, she guessed.

"She's a pretty child. You don't need to have her looking any kind of way."

"I wasn't. I was going to take her to the beauty salon."

"What? Why?"

"I can't do it."

"Her hair is easy to do. You just lazy." Sparrow started to pick up her barrettes and yarn ties off the ground. Carole came running out and up to Sparrow and hugged her. "You welcome, precious."

"Leave my child alone. Get on out of here. We're fine."

The girl ran back to her father.

"Where is her mother?"

The man's bear like stance calmed down and he sat on a porch swing. "She died. About 18 months ago. Car accident."

"I'm sorry," Sparrow said softly. "I really am."

"Been doing the best that I can by myself, but between my job and here, time goes by."

"I'm used to taking care of kids. I can help. You all just moved here?"

The man looked up at her and appraised her, coolly, up and down.

Sparrow shivered.

He didn't seem to like what he saw. "You don't need to worry about it. Go ahead. Thank you for the hair. I can pay you." He reached into a pocket and pulled out a five-dollar bill. "There. Thanks. Carole is fine."

"Is she deaf?"

"No, she's not deaf. She's just.... get out of here. Mind your own business. Get out before I call the authorities."

Some people might look at him and call him handsome, but not Sparrow. With his thick eyebrows all scrunched up in the middle of his forehead, his bearing came across to her like a fortress—a muscular block, covered in mahogany red-brown skin. His thick lips were twisted into an upside-down frown. This dude had to be over 30, someone a person of her age would not trust. "Fine. Stop being such a grouch. I was just worried."

"No need to worry about her. She's my problem."

Sparrow collected her purse and walked down the walkway. She glanced over her shoulder at the man as he ventured back into the house. She knew that Carole's lovely eyes were following her, and in some way, she knew there was sorrow behind those eyes.

Sparrow knew sorrow well.

CHAPTER FOUR

She had just gotten her high school diploma so there was no way Sparrow was trying to be the one who would end up in jail. Oh, how her mother would love that. But for the rest of that Saturday, during the night and into the next morning, she couldn't help but think of Carole's delighted expression over her hair and the one of horror at her father.

Still, when Sparrow learned Carole had lost her mother, there was a pain that struck her in her middle. So, when the morning came and it was time to make the oatmeal, she put on her dungarees and slipped outside, quickly walking to Carole's house.

What would she do? Knock on the door? What about Carole's father? She remembered how his brown arms bulged in his tee shirt. His close cropped afro and mustache were very appealing to someone who saw him whenever he was in his right mind, she supposed.

She imagined the magnitude of his anger if she kidnapped his child.

I'm not kidnapping her. I'm inviting her for breakfast and church. That's all.

In her hand, Sparrow carried a note, hurriedly scribbled, to let Carole's know that she wasn't kidnapping his child.

Her heart pounded at the thought of confronting the angry, sad man. But there was a cord, something inside of her pulling her to save that child. Carole's mother would want her child to be taken care of better.

And the way Carole's face lit up like a sun when she sang to her, filled Sparrow with joy. Maybe the little girl could do something in the play. She could be someone, too.

Sparrow stood in front of the house and faced it... nothing to it, but to do it.

She charged up the walkway and peered into the side door. There, in the kitchen stood Carole. She was dressed in pink pajamas and was standing at the stove perched up on her toes on top of a few thick books, peering at something in a pot.

Sparrow knocked lightly on the door. Carole turned to her, looking alarmed for a second. Then she descended and came running to the door, her neat pigtails that Sparrow made flew out behind her in a pleasing way.

The girl remembered her. Sparrow's heart danced as Carole opened the door, then stood there in her slightly silent way.

"Good morning to you on this Lord's Day, honey. Are you making breakfast?"

Carole nodded.

Sparrow stepped into the kitchen and looked at the pot, filled with water. There was no food in it yet, but there was a bag of grits on the table.

"Where is your father, honey? Isn't he helping you?"

Carole shook her head and laid down on her hands to show that he was still sleeping.

A bolt of anger surged through Sparrow. Why didn't he get up when this child got up? What kind of father was he?

She swallowed hard and bent down to whisper to Carole, "How about you come to my house for pancakes, and then come to church with me?"

Carole's little face lit up, then just as quickly, she looked downcast.

"I have a note. I will leave it for your father so he won't be concerned, ok?"

The girl looked eager again.

"Go put on a pretty dress and we will get going."

Sparrow sat herself at the table in the kitchen and looked around. The house needed a good cleaning. One of those things, she guessed, was missing a woman's touch. Maybe if she became friends with the girl, she would be able to show her what to do. Carole couldn't be any older than her brothers. How would she know?

When Carole emerged, she had on a pocket dress that was a nice orange color, but it was too tight. It probably was a dress her mama bought for her before she died.

The sharp prick of tears struck, but Sparrow smiled at her. "How pretty you look. And I know I have some orange yarn ties at home for you. Come on."

She relished the feel of Carole's trusting hand in hers on the walk home. Her heart pounded with each step that she took from the Claiborne house, or whatever the name was now. She enjoyed pointing out the trees and houses with the young girl who seemed to be listening. Her father said she wasn't deaf so she wondered what was wrong with her. No matter. She would keep speaking and saying anything to see the light in Carole's eyes.

When they arrived at her house, she found Beatrix had put the oatmeal on. In defiance, Sparrow pushed past her gathering up the milk, flour, eggs and sugar to make pancakes.

"What are you doing?" her sister asked her.

"I'm making pancakes."

"You know Mama ain't going to like that."

"We have a special guest this Lord's Day. Carole, have a seat."

Beatrix threw her hands up and marched from the kitchen.

Sparrow knew she was going to tell, but she didn't care. *Heifer*.

No need to throw away the oatmeal. She put it in the batter and greased up a couple of skillets. She pinned a tea towel on Carole and the small child stood on a chair helping to stir the mixture.

"Well, well, what do we have here?"

"Good morning, Mama," Sparrow greeted. "We have a special guest. This is our new neighbor, Miss Carole."

Faitha nodded to the child and gave what Sparrow thought of as a grimace. "Welcome, Miss Carole. I would like to speak to Miss Sparrow here for a minute, if I may."

Sparrow gave her mother a look.

Faitha stared back at her. The death stare.

"I'll be right back, Carole."

Fortunately, Candy came sailing into the room at just the right moment and Sparrow was able to ask her baby sister to keep an eye on the pancake making. Candy loved pancakes, so it was no problem to step out onto the front porch of their ramshackle house and speak to her mother.

Sparrow wiped her hands on her apron.

"Whose child is that?"

"They just moved to the neighborhood. I'm bringing her to church."

"Well that's good, given that you are just a recent convert yourself. But why feed her? This ain't no way station."

That's what this was about? *Money*. "I can pay you. I'll add a little extra to my contribution."

Faitha opened her mouth, but something stopped her from speaking. For once. "Fine."

Of course, her mother made sure to have a hearty portion of pancakes with brown sugar syrup that they made, so they didn't have to buy any.

There was a mad scramble to get ready for church while they listened to a black radio station playing a song by the Mighty Clouds of Joy.

Sparrow sang as she donned her slip and a pink sleeveless shift with her white shoes and purse. She wasn't a clotheshorse, but she did like to look nice. The tightness of Carole's dress irritated her more. There might be something in the church cupboard for her. If not, Sparrow could dip into her small savings and buy some fabric. Beatrix sewed. Sparrow didn't, but she would be willing to learn to help the young girl get some better clothes.

The family had a merry walk to church, but when it was time for Sparrow to go up into the choir loft to sing, Carole started to yank and pull on her. Sparrow bent down and tried to explain, but Faitha sighed. "Ain't nothing for it but for her to go on up there with you. She'll behave."

Faitha walked away from her with a satisfied little smile on her face. "Now you know what it feels like to be a mother, with children on you all the time. Praise God for a lesson."

Sparrow was the choir director, and there wasn't anything for it. So, Carole sat up in a chair in the front, with the entire church looking on her as they sang the hymns and anthems, *Can't Nobody Do It Like He Can* and *Oh Happy Day*.

Carole seemed to love that one. She clapped, swayed, and moved her lips as the choir stomped it out. Sparrow's heart lifted in joy to see that child celebrating the Lord in front of the entire church. It sure helped them to get happy as well.

It did Sparrow's heart a world of good to see her happy.

The song was about to wind down when the church doors opened and a tall, broad shouldered, handsome man stepped into the back row. Reverend Parrish preached on, but clearly, the attention of the congregation was diverted from the military man who slipped into the back row.

She peered at the man a bit, but he was quite a distance away. Then she realized that the man in the uniform was Carole's father, all dressed up and looking completely different than he did yesterday.

Carole waggled her fingers at her daddy and it took everything in Sparrow not to slide down in her seat.

When he spotted his daughter, he had the grace to come down the side aisle closer to them and sat at the end of the row on her side, glaring at her for the remainder of the service. His anger at her was so blatant, he didn't seem to notice that every other woman in the church had their eyes on him. The interested glare.

No, his, *I want to kill you,* glare was for Sparrow only, and not in a good way.

She gulped being under his notice so much.

Faitha was staring at him until she saw that he was staring at Sparrow so hard. Then the look on her face relaxed and her mother sat there with a sly smirk on her face. Faitha was the kind of mother who liked for life to teach her children lessons. There was nothing so satisfying to her as to stand back and watch her child get hit upside the head.

When the Reverend asked for people with changed hearts to come forward and be blessed and no one did, Sparrow stood up and immediately went into the choir room with Carole in hand, lest her father come back and confront her directly.

"You should go out to see your father," Sparrow said. "He came to get you. He misses you. If want to come to camp, you should ask him."

Carole's eyebrows pitched up.

"I think you can talk. If you want to."

Carole shook her head.

But Sparrow nodded. "You can. You've just decided not to. When you want to say something, you will. If you want it bad enough."

Her eyebrows drew together and Carole ducked out between a couple of choir members.

Whew. That was done. She had plenty to do here to check on the proceedings for tomorrow.

Her fellow choir members were eager to get on with their Sunday afternoon and departed quickly. Sparrow stayed in the room cleaning up and organizing folders.

The door opened and Carole emerged holding her father's hand.

"There you are. What do you mean taking my child out of our house? I ought to turn you over to the police."

Sparrow stilled her thudding heart by crossing her arms over her chest. "I ought to turn you over for neglect," she responded. "I saw her trying to make her own breakfast, all alone, on a hot stove. She might have burned the house down while you slept."

The large man with the imposing physique backed up from her. "Who do you think you are? Telling me about what I do."

"Her dress is too small, too. More neglect."

Here came his twisted-up brow and frown face again, like he looked when she first met him. "Leave us alone, Bird woman. You hear me? Carole is none of your business. She's mine. Stay away from us or I will call the police. Ain't no one taking Carole from me. *No one.*"

His insistence was scary, but Sparrow knew she was in God's house. She refused to back down for what she believed in.

He picked Carole up and started to carry her away. Her small face bounced on her father's shoulder and her arms stuck out toward Sparrow.

The man stopped and a guttural, metallic sound rose from the little girl, rusty from disuse. "Sparrow!"

CHAPTER FIVE

Peeking in on the church service, John Charles St. Clair had never seen such a sight as Sparrow, taking the lead on *Oh Happy Day*. It was as if a beam of light burst through and there was sun in his life again. He wasn't an especially religious man, but now he understood how that was entirely possible. Second Missionary Baptist must do a regular conversion of the heathen with an earth-bound angel like Sparrow Jones in the choir.

He couldn't let it get to him. He couldn't let her get to him.

Although the sight of Carole up in the choir loft in her creamsicle dress slapping a tambourine in time to the beat wearing a big smile on her face was just about all he needed to run up to the front of the church and proclaim God's mercy on him.

Still, something held him back. Some hard, cold force in his heart kept him from the acceptance. From the love.

Part of it had to do with the fact that he didn't know how long he had in this world to enjoy love. What was the point of embracing that happiness and sweetness when 1968 could be his last year on earth? That his little girl could easily be without a father within a year? Carole as an orphan? No, it was better that he just gut out the rest of his life. All because of the United States Army, his life was theirs. Precious little he could do about it now. How ironic that he joined the military as a too young and scared teenage father trying to find a better way to support his child and Dina, his wife. The very thing that gave him a steady hand, guidance and a paycheck had turned around on him and asked for his life in return. He had no choice but to give it.

When Sparrow Jones dared to step to him, wrenching his child from his arms, getting Carole to finally speak after a year of silence, that was the last straw.

Who was this woman, this unearthly force with boy hair, slender and skinny with a stronger fighting spirit than any form of general he had ever come across?

Carole went right to her, as if she knew her, as if she belonged in the woman's arms... away from him.

His heart divided in two. One half was Carole's. She knew that. The other was this dark ugly force that meant that he had to keep her protected from anything that she didn't know.

It was that half that won out, pulling his daughter from the strange woman's arms, his actions drawing a crowd outside of the choir room.

"Are you ok?" His voice came gruff, roughed out with emotion, hating how it showed in front of this stranger.

"Ok? Did you hear her? Oh, I'm so proud of you, Carole!"

Everyone quieted as the little girl strained to speak again. There was immediate silence. Everyone wanted to hear more, but Carole croaked and a look of pure frustration came across her face.

"I'm going to take her to the doctor on the base."

"What for?" Sparrow's forehead creased into a maze of confusion.

"She can talk. Something is wrong that she can't do it again." He knew he sounded ridiculous. He just wanted to get his daughter out of there, away from the prying eyes, away from this angel being who was stealing his valuable time with his precious daughter.

Sparrow spread her hands out so gracefully, he wondered if they were wings. "People, please. Let Miss Carole have some breathing room and space."

And just like that, every being—people who were probably three times the age of this slip of a young woman, scattered. Just like that, she had reached into him and knew what he needed. Within a minute, the three of them stood in the hallway. Alone.

He pressed his daughter to his chest again, lifting her up, supporting her with his hands. Carole leaned into him, her head on his shoulder, just where she should be.

"I thank you."

"I did nothing. It was Carole. She knew she would talk when she had something to say."

Sparrow reached her hand out to stroke Carole's back, but he stepped away from her touch.

There was a strange look in her eyes that he couldn't read, but then, the general was back again.

He spoke for them. "We'll be just fine. Thank you for bringing her to church. I would prefer to be asked first, but thank you. She won't be bothering you again."

"Carole is no bother. As a matter-of-fact , she probably has something else to ask you."

JC felt a slight alarm and pulled back so he could see Carole's face. The look there was blank, but then she parted her lips and said, "Sck."

"It's ok, Carole."

She shook her head so fast that the braids spun rapidly, hitting her in her face. "Schoo."

"School?" Sparrow said.

Carole looked happy again, nodding her head up and down.

School. That would take place in the fall, when he had to be away from her. He had thoughts about some kind of boarding school where someone would look over her. Maybe a special school where they would help her with her speaking, but, he hadn't gotten to that yet. He was just trying to look out for her right now.

Still, watching this young woman, how she interpreted for his child, was a lesson in itself. How she did it, he didn't know. But the connection between them tore at him and he couldn't explain why.

"I'm having a school here at the church for the summer, Mr...."

"St. Clair."

"Mr. St. Clair Carole wants to come. We feed them breakfast and lunch and then she can come home at 1:00 p.m. There will be Bible study, of course, music and at the end of the summer there will be a pageant."

"A pageant."

"A play. All of the children will put on a play to show what they've learned over the summer, which I've centered around the history of our people. I still don't have a title though."

What was she talking about? Pageants? Like Miss America? "Carole wouldn't be able to do that kind of thing."

"Yes, she could. If she doesn't want to perform in the play, she can help me. I will need all the help I can get with nearly a hundred children in the camp."

"Are you running it?"

"Yes, I am."

"How old are you anyway?"

A flash came across her face. "I really don't see why that matters."

"You seem young to be in charge of running a camp."

"I've been the assistant for the past three years. I'm running the camp in Mrs. Lincoln's stead. She's expecting."

"I see."

"You must let her come. I'll come for her in the morning myself."

Sparrow reached out again to the girl, but he wasn't quick enough. His daughter wriggled out of his hold and went to Sparrow, where it looked as if they were having a party just for two.

Could he win this battle? This woman had conqueror stamped all over her, but he was Carole's father. He had to do something. "I will bring her. What time does this camp open?"

"8:30 tomorrow morning."

"We'll be here. Bright and early."

"You are going to come here?" Her face was all scrunched up.

"Carole *is* my daughter. I'll make sure she is properly supervised."

"Men don't usually…." Sparrow stopped herself. "Ok. That's fine. We're going home for lunch. Bologna sandwiches. Nothing special. She's welcome. I mean, you are welcome to join us."

JC captured his daughter's hand. Enough was enough. "No thank you. We have food at home. Come, Carole."

The young girl, his daughter, seemed to grow roots from her feet and stay firmly planted in the ground. She wouldn't come. How much more betrayal could he endure?

"Hey, Carole." Sparrow bent down to his child, whispered something in her ear and within seconds her feet were free. She waved at the slip of a woman.

"Bye." Her small voice came, clearer, less tiny stronger. She squeezed his hand as if she understood what he wanted and they walked off out of a side door. He could see his house in the distance and he quickly guided his daughter to it not completely sure if he were doing the right thing.

"Magic," Carole said.

Yes. She had that right for sure.

For the first time in nearly two years, JC was looking forward to tomorrow.

♩♩♩

Sparrow watched as the two walked off. The bond between herself and the little girl pulled tightly. Would she have something good enough to eat? Would she have to make it? He was her father after all, but she wanted to make sure.

She turned to the door and opened it and nearly every member of the congregation of Second Missionary was at the door straining to hear as if their lives depended on it, waiting for her to come out. The questions came thick and fast.

"What happened, Sparrow?"

"Is the baby going to be okay?"

"Who is that man?"

"Look. Everything is alright people. Go home. Eat your lunch. Y'all get the juicy gossip later."

Several of the church members gave her hard looks. She glared right back at them. Church people were always getting into stuff that was not their business. They all dwindled away, even the Reverend. He knew better than to give her a rough time. The only one that was left behind was her mother.

"What was that all about, Sparrow? Do you know that man?"

"He's Carole's father. What else do I need to know?"

Faitha fanned herself and she took on a different look on her face that she didn't recognize. What was it?

"Little Carole's daddy certainly cut a fine figure in that uniform."

"Mother!"

"Well he did. Don't tell me you didn't notice."

"I didn't."

"I birthed you into this world, Sparrow Jones. Don't even try it. You ain't dead. You noticed him and he noticed you."

"He noticed me?"

"Girl, yes. Everyone in the church felt the tension between y'all. You just a young thing, not knowing what you need to know. I'm not displeased. He being in the military, that's an opportunity. You can see the world. He be taking care of you. Got a steady check coming in." Faitha crossed her arms and nodded her head. "Maybe there's something for you yet, girlie."

"I'm worried about little Carole."

Her mother leaned down, looking as if she almost wanted to laugh at her. "Girl, don't you know the best way to get to a man is through his child? Don't act like I didn't tell you that. I know that I did."

Sparrow glared at her mother. "You were always too busy getting your own boyfriends to ever talk to me or teach me anything."

Faitha's face took on her own hard gaze. "I did what I had to do to make a way for you and your sisters and brothers. Everything I ever did was to keep clothes on your back and food in your mouth, Miss. Just you remember that when you make a way with your military man. See, I can't even be mad that you would dare to be so disrespectful to me. One day, you gone thank me for all I taught you. One day."

Sparrow doubted it. Still, as Faitha walked away from her, corralling her sons to get them on home, with Beatrix and Candy following, she hated that she felt like crying. Never, in all her life, had she felt so completely mixed up about so many things. She needed to be somewhere to prepare for everything: the school, the children, and encountering John Charles St. Clair again.

CHAPTER SIX

He had upped for only two tours of duty so far, but what Sparrow Jones pulled off was nothing short of a miracle. Any parent who thought they were going to drop off their child and leave were wrong. She wrung every ounce of guilt and shame in them. If they wanted to drop a child off, they had to promise to bring home baked cookies, make punch, or promise cloth for costumes for the pageant at the end. Sparrow passed out rectangles of construction paper that were a kind of code for what the parents would do. When he came with Carole, he got a purple rectangle. He looked around. He didn't see any other purples. Lots of people were walking away with blue, green or red ones.

"What does this mean?" He held it up.

"Go inside. You'll find out."

Carole squeezed his hand, after she reached out and got a hug from Sparrow. "Come on, Daddy."

What did this woman have in store for him? Did he really want to know?

Sparrow wore close fitting dungarees, white flats and a sleeveless blue top, but her benign appearance belied the brusque, no nonsense way she pulled together the operations of the school. Besides, it was probably better to go inside and see what she was talking about, rather than focusing on her snug bottom in those dungarees she wore. The less he knew about that, and the way her short boy haircut curled at the edges of her neck, the better.

He followed Carole into the church's basement and two young women were inside doling out bowls of oatmeal to the children. He held up his purple rectangle and got tied into an apron and told to pour milk for his efforts. What? He wasn't a nanny. He wasn't there to wipe children's mouths or clean up after them. But when he saw Carole sit down at a table with some little girls, he realized that she needed friends of her own age. So he continued to pour, wipe up tables and take bowls to the sink where some mothers greeted him with sly smiles as they washed the dishes clean in hot soapy water.

Thirty minutes flew by before he knew what had happened. He heard Sparrow's whistle and he came out to see her standing there with the Reverend, and she said, "Welcome to the first day of camp. Reverend Parrish will lead us in prayer first, and then we will get started. Bow your head and fold your hands and let's ask God's blessing on this happening."

What had he wandered into? What was this all about? He had just come here to drop off his child. He hadn't expected all of this. How had this little woman upended his world in such a short amount of time?

Given what was about to happen to him, he didn't even know if he believed in God. Carole came beside him and slipped her hand in his. He watched the top of her head drop and those twisty braids Sparrow had put into her head bounced up and down gently. They were still tied off with creamsicle-colored yarn bows. She looked so pretty. Before he knew it, he had dropped his own head and closed his eyes, relishing the feel of Carole's small hand in his, imprinting the feel of it in his mind, trying to think of anything other than the horrors he faced where he would be asked to fight a war he didn't understand.

When the Reverend was through, Sparrow blew her whistle and there was instant quiet. "When you all came in, I hung a ribbon with a certain color around your neck. I want you to go find the adult who has the color square you do. That's going to be your teacher for the summer. We will come together for our opening convocation and then we will break off for the day's activities."

All of a sudden, Carole had slipped away from him and went up to Sparrow, who had a light blue rectangle that matched his daughter.

This was not what he had planned! He was there to supervise Carole, not some other people's children. In an instance, he was surrounded by a group of boys including Sparrow's identical twin brothers.

He wasn't there to teach! What had this woman done? He tried to make his way to get closer to her, but the circle of children tightened around him.

Where was his whistle to help him keep order in this crazy world? How would he stop this madness?

Glancing across the room in his horror, he saw a sly gaze slip across Sparrow's face and she gave him a slight smile. Oh, she thought she had won this round? Well, he would show her. He started to step forward, when one of the boys, who couldn't have been more than five, looked up at him with large, trusting eyes. "What's your name, Mister?"

Once that happened, he was lost. The day flew by on Sparrow's wings. Literally. She had declared it Carter G. Woodson week and the children learned about how Negro History week was created back in 1926. Because it was a week that had taken place during February, Sparrow served homemade Jello Popsicles and graham crackers as a snack.

Before he knew it, he was sitting on the floor next to Carole, wanting to take a nap because he was exhausted.

Sparrow came into the lower basement, clapping her hands, getting folks to straighten up to be ready the next day. There really wasn't much to do because she and the other teachers had taught the children to clean up after themselves.

JC held up a hand. "Let me get this straight. You were so desperate for teachers that you felt you had to con me into being one."

"Well, no, Mr. St. Clair. But someone couldn't show this morning, so you had to be a replacement. You're off the hook for tomorrow. You can be one of the drop off parents bringing boxes of graham crackers or bolts of cloth for the pageant, if you like. But, we really need you in the classroom with these boys who don't see a male figure like yourself often. My brothers, for instance, don't deal with their father much. So, I wanted you to know how much I appreciate that you stepped in. Thank you."

Her eyes were so serious, he had to wave a hand. "No. It's ok. It's not a problem."

"You'll come back tomorrow?"

"I didn't say all that."

"Well, you've got to let me know. Tomorrow is music day."

"Music day?"

"Yes. I've got to get the children used to the music for the pageant. So it's music day every Tuesday."

"Sounds like Mickey Mouse Club or something."

"I was a faithful watcher. Were you?"

"Sometimes. I think I'm quite a bit older than you, so I wasn't their target audience."

"How old are you anyway?"

"How old do you think I am?" JC stood up and towered over her, as if to emphasize his age.

"Thirty?"

"I'm not thirty. I'm twenty-four."

"Oh. Ok. You just seemed old. I'm sorry."

"Everyone seems old when you are eighteen."

"That's what they say." She flashed her clipboard and smiled.

She marched off and he had to look away from watching how her dungarees fit snug on her backside... again.

Carole squeezed his hand. He squeezed her hand back. "Ok, honey. We'll go home and relax. This camp is a sure cure for insomnia."

His daughter giggled. Giggled? Carole? He folded his work apron up and laid it on a table, ready to take his daughter home for some peace and quiet.

♩♩♩

She didn't expect to see him anymore. He now understood where she was coming from and didn't mean Carole any harm; she was fine with him sending Carole down the street to the camp every day.

Now that she knew that though, she wanted to see him.

When she got home, Faitha said, "Did that little girl's handsome daddy come?"

"He did, Mama, and he was one of the teachers," Beatrix piped up, opening the icebox to get cool from the June heat.

"Pay her no mind. I was busy trying to coordinate this camp. I have no time for such foolishness. He's handsome, sure, but I have my job to do and he did his job, helping with the boys."

She walked out of the kitchen to go to her room to change her clothes and she heard her mother and sister's loud guffaws behind her. She didn't care. She had done what she needed to do. It felt good to get that child into the neighborhood activities. She would be playing with the other children in no time.

She hummed the tune to *This Little Light o' Mine* the tune for the week. All the children would come together at the end in their costumes and sing the song.

She wondered if JC St. Clair would show up to help her. But why was he on military leave for the summer? Had he done something wrong in his job? No matter what his reasoning was, she would make sure that this summer was a summer for Carole to enjoy herself.

She was thrilled the next morning when he showed up, with Carole in hand.

"Are you going to stay?"

"Miss Sparrow, you must be looking to wear me out."

"I just don't want to interfere with your job. I know that takes priority."

Just when she thought that she was making some headway with him, a shadow came over his face. "I'm available this summer. So I'll be here to help you to the end of the program."

"I appreciate that, Mr. St. Clair. I need all the help I can get." Sparrow tried to keep her voice light, so that the darkness didn't return.

"Look, I'm shipping out to 'Nam in September. I want to make as many memories with Carole as I can. Before I have to leave."

Sparrow felt as if she had been slammed into a hard glass window. Stunned. Air filtered into her head. "But why? They can't ship you out because you have your daughter."

"I'm afraid they can."

"Even though she has no other parent. That's one more reason that the war is unfair. Who do we have to write? What has to be said to keep you here?"

His eyes fixed on her in confusion. "I'm sworn to duty in the military. That's my job."

"You were sworn to duty with Carole when she was born."

"You don't know how Carole was born. It was a time of upheaval in my life. I was only 16 years old."

"Oh my." Sparrow's eyes, and body were immediately downcast.

"You really should keep to your own business." He seemed more amused when he said this. There was nothing funny in this situation to Sparrow.

"It's hard to do that when you are telling me that you have to leave this little girl behind. Will she stay with your family?"

"My family cut me off when I told them Carole was coming. Told me I was grown enough to make a child, so I had to get out."

"Wow," she murmured. "I thought my mother was tough."

The look he gave her was one of complete disgust. It was the way he had looked at her before he knew her. The way she thought he had stopped looking at her. Now it was back.

"Miss Sparrow, you are so, so young. Excuse me. I'll go inside and get started."

He left her behind, standing there, holding her clipboard, clutching it, worrying the edges of her organizing pages, leaving her behind without a clue about how to start with him again.

CHAPTER SEVEN

The distance between them kept up over the next few weeks. Sparrow didn't seem to know what to say to him anymore. He had to know she was adamantly opposed to the war. The war was a white man's war where they were comfortable using Black bodies in their stead so they didn't have to die. "I don't see why Carole has to lose her daddy for a white man's foolishness."

Faitha peered at her as they fried their family's chicken contribution for the Independence Day picnic. It was the one day that Sparrow was off. Their town gathered in the square for the celebration, parade, and the fireworks. She tried to approach JC several times to ask what they were doing for the holiday, but he always evaded her.

"It's not really your business, Sparrow."

"Now here you go. I'm just saying. They are a for real reason why this war needs to come to an end. It's terrible."

"So what are you going to do?"

"I'm going to go over there and I'm going to ask him if they have enough food for a basket. If they don't, they can share with us."

"I love how you offer up my food."

"You know I contribute, Mama. Don't start."

"Ok. Then what?"

"I have no idea." Sparrow took off her apron. "I'm going over there now."

"Don't be surprised if he tosses you right out. He has a right to spend his summer with his daughter as he sees fit."

"I'm just asking if they have enough food."

"Are you sure that's why you are going over there?"

"Mama, I think you are the one who has a thing for him."

"Who wouldn't, as fine as he looks in his uniform? He's mighty handsome. But I just want you to be real clear about why you going over there."

Sparrow bunched up her apron. "I'm going to be right back."

"Humph," Faitha said.

It was better to go over there earlier rather than later anyway. The skies were a little clouded over, but the news report said that it would be clear later on. As it was, it was hot enough, as the beginning of July in Georgia should be. When she got to the old Claiborne, now St. Clair house, she could feel a fine sheen of dampness on her forehead and in her sleeveless armpits. She knocked on the door and Carole came to the front door and embraced her tightly.

"Where is your daddy?"

"In. Here." Carole's speech was coming along better, but she still halted in the way she spoke. Regardless, Sparrow was glad that she spoke.

She went inside of the house, seeking out John Charles who was in the middle of washing up some dishes. For some reason, he looked extremely appealing washing the dishes. "Miss. Jones. What's going on?"

His deep voice was very polite, but distant. Carole pulled up a chair, hanging onto every word Sparrow said. "The Independence Day celebration is down at the park. Everyone brings a basket and there is a program and fireworks. Mama was frying chicken and she wanted to make sure you all had a basket to come and eat dinner with us."

"Thank you for the invitation, but we have hot dogs."

"You don't want any of my mother's fried chicken?"

He smiled. It was the first smile she had seen on him in weeks. Well wonders do happen.

"Well, then you'll have to come or I'm not bringing you guys any. Or I'll bring Carole some and she will eat it in front of you."

"That's just cruel, Sparrow. Very cruel." He was still smiling, showing a set of beautiful teeth. He had a lovely smile that gleamed like a sun in his chiseled features.

"You haven't said my name in a long time."

"I'm sorry."

"I thought you were mad at me."

His rippled chest rose and fell in a sigh. "I'm not mad at anyone. I'm mad at something."

She reached out to him, touching his arm. "It seems so unfair. I've been protesting for about a year now. What a powerful thing it would be if you...."

"Don't, Sparrow. Please." He turned from her, looking as if he were going to the steps to call Carole. "I want some homemade fried chicken, ok? Please."

His pleas struck her in a way that nothing had before. This man might be having his last summer in this world. He didn't need to hear her going on and on about the protests. He needed to have a good summer.

Even though she didn't believe in his cause, and more deeply believed in her right to protest him, she would do that. She watched him climb the steps in his shorts, appreciating the view, and then sank down in a chair. *What is wrong with me*?

It might be one of the hardest things she had ever done. She had never willingly been quiet about anything before. But there was something larger at stake here now than what she had to say. She had to help this man, who was a good if not grumpy man, to make memories for his daughter. Carole was a sweet girl, but if she lost her will to speak when her mother died; what might happen to her if something happened to her father?

In that instant, when Carole came running downstairs to her in her nightgown and padding around on bare feet, she knew she had a purpose. Music school would be wonderful, but if she could make this summer one to remember, she might help make things easier for Carole.

Now she understood what mattered.

♩♩♩

The combination of Sparrow and fresh homemade fried chicken was too much to resist. Sparrow's mother Faitha was not one of his favorite people, but it had been so long since he had that food, he was willing to put up with her staring at him as if he were a prize bull.

Besides, a day of fun would be worth it if Sparrow was there.

Not that it meant anything, but he just liked to watch her move, be in charge, hug Carole and bend down to talk to her face to face. These moments were like Kodak snaps kept in his mind. He knew he would need every one of those snaps to pull out if he were to get through this assignment alive.

Maybe the more snaps JC made, the more protection he might have from the enemies' bullets.

He liked the thought.

So he played the gallant all day. He helped to carry items to the park. He spread the blankets and erected a large yellow umbrella with tassels on it if people wanted to eat underneath. Several of the kids from the program came up to him and while the ladies got the food ready, he showed them a game of touch football. The exercise felt good and the kids, especially Sparrow's brothers, seemed to enjoy it.

When the food was laid out on the table, he helped himself to a plate. And another. And another.

Sparrow's mother laughed as she continued to make him plates.

At the last, JC just couldn't anymore. She tried to urge him to take more cherry pie, but he couldn't. Still, it was all so good.

He noticed Sparrow was not eating. "You eat like a bird," he couldn't resist saying.

Sparrow fixed him with a look. "Very funny. Besides, birds eat four times their weight. Imagine what I would look like if I did that."

He pointed a finger in her direction. Her face wasn't as animated as it usually was.

"Is there something wrong?"

"I don't usually like to eat too much before I perform."

"You're performing? What?"

"The National Anthem. I have to admit, since learning more about you, this is the first time that I've thought through the words and what they mean."

"Oh. I see."

Sparrow leaned in. "I hope that you like it. I'll sing it just for you."

She turned and walked away.

Wow. He didn't expect that from her. He was honored, just as much as he was shocked by her offer. He was a nobody. Still, it was nice to believe that someone else besides Carole might miss him when he...

No. He couldn't give power to that thought. He watched as Sparrow made her way to the grandstand in front of the crowd.

The crowd was filled with Black people. That was because once they integrated this gathering about five years ago, white people stayed at home or visited one another's homes. They didn't come to the park anymore. Some of them did, especially the children, but they stayed far away. Once that happened, the Black people made their own program, doing what they wanted to do.

So they would hire a jazz band to play music. Sometimes, some of the younger people tried to smuggle in a portable record player to listen to James Brown, but without any microphones to blast it, they would have to crowd around a table to do their dances like the frug or the watusi. He wasn't up on the latest dances.

Sparrow probably was. Still, he didn't see Sparrow going over there and wondered why she wasn't interested in the dancing. Still, he watched her make her way, dressed in a sleeveless apricot colored top and her white dungarees, to the front of the crowd. When she did and she stood on top of some old wooden boxes, he was startled at her bravery. Her power. Her glory.

Everyone, young and old, stopped whatever they were doing to watch her. So did he.

"Welcome all. We're having a great day here, enjoying one another's company. But before I sing the National Anthem, I want to say something. I know it would surprise you all to know, knowing how I have felt about the war, to say this, but I want to dedicate this song to those who are fighting in Vietnam."

The sound of Sparrow's voice was punctuated by the sound of murmurs in the crowd.

"Yes. I mean it. There has been too much loss lately. First Martin Luther King, Jr. Then Bobby Kennedy. I've said my say because there has been so much loss. I want it to stop. Still, I know now that people are going over there because they have been forced to by the government. So we really should think more about their sacrifice. We should honor that sacrifice. That's how I want to celebrate this Independence Day. With honor."

The quiet of the hot July day wrapped around them, before Sparrow launched into the first notes of the *Star-Spangled Banner*. Listening to her sing was like hearing the song for the first time. Her bright, clear voice echoed into the summer day and it was almost as if he could see each note hanging in the air before it reached his ears, and reached into his soul, leaving her imprint there. Her song and the way she sang it was proof. This woman was meant to be a part of his life, no matter how long or short it would be.

It had been a long time since JC had believed in a higher power... too long. There had been too much loss in his life lately to believe otherwise. But the stirring he had when he saw Carole praying, came upon him again. Sparrow was meant to be with him somehow. He might only have a few months left but it was up to him to make the most of it with her.

He closed his eyes. It seemed to be the only right thing to do in this moment that was... holy. "Please. Help me. Help me make the most of this time. Help me to make a memory I can carry with me into battle. Cover over these wounds in my heart and help me be brave and strong. In the name of God."

Because love required bravery. Almost as much bravery needed going to war.

He was ready.

CHAPTER EIGHT

Sparrow was well used to the people of her small town giving her compliments on her singing. She had heard them ever since she was a little girl who aspired to sing for John F. Kennedy, then for Bobby Kennedy. The same words of praise came to her today. But today was different. Even Faitha never said much of anything to her about her singing.

When she got back to the table after the crowds of people had congratulated her, Faitha sat there, shaking her head. "Well done, daughter."

"Thank you, Mama."

She had always thought that when her mother would give her the praise she had long sought, she would feel whole somehow. More complete. Now the words slid from her, like drips of cooking oil. It didn't make her feel much of anything, only sad that it took so long for her mother to acknowledge her gift.

"Well, there. Would you like some pie?"

Sparrow knew that was Faitha's way of saying she was sorry for all the years that she didn't give her praise. It was Faitha's way of saying I love you.

"Sure, Mama. Thanks."

Faitha got busy cutting her a slice of peach, a narrow one, just for her.

Then JC approached her. "That singing was something special today. Thank you."

"I'm glad that you liked it."

They stood there in companionable silence. "I hope that you want to do something with that one day. You have a gift."

"Oh. I've had dreams. When I was a girl, I wanted to sing for the President. But then he was killed. Then his brother, who I thought would be the president I would sing for. Then someone killed him. So now, I hope for music school."

"I think with a voice like that, you can do it all. You can aim higher. You don't have to settle for teaching children spirituals."

"I don't think that's settling. It's important work. If we don't pass those songs onto our children, they will lose them. They are the songs of our heritage."

"I always thought of them as sorrow songs. Sad songs."

Sparrow bristled. "They aren't. When I think about it, I think of them as songs that they created. It's their art. It's the way they showed their humanity under brutal conditions when they weren't allowed to have even that."

She thought her defensive posture would make him angry. Instead, he lowered his head and nodded as if he understood. "I had a tough upbringing. I used to have a notebook and I would write down my thoughts. Phrases. One day, someone stole it from me and I never kept one again."

She couldn't help herself. The hurt in his face was so obvious, she reached out to him and touched his arm. "Now you are a grown man, Mr. St. Clair. You can start it again. You have a gift too."

He placed his palm on top of her hand. Strength and feeling pulsed there. "Thank you for the suggestion."

The jazz band was playing a quieter song in the twilight.

"Care to take a stroll?"

"With me?"

"Sure, why not?"

"Carole, she..." Sparrow turned and she saw Carole sitting with her sisters on a blanket. Both Beatrix and Candy looked unhappy.

They both laughed.

"Clearly, Carole is the one doing the babysitting."

"I know. Both of them want to get away from Mama and go chasing after boys. Carole looks like she has them in control."

"Well?"

Sparrow tucked her arm into the crook of his. His arm felt like granite, but the skin there was soft and smooth. "Sure."

JC escorted her toward the music and offered his hand.

"I'm not the best dancer." Sparrow lowered her head.

"Please, Miss Jones. Your musical talent is evident. Come on. I will lead the way."

JC swept her in his arms. She took in a deep breath. Even at her prom, she danced with several young men. This was not a young man. JC was a real man. "You ok?"

She shook her head as if she were clearing it. "I'm fine."

"Yes, you are." He smiled down at her and they danced back and forth on the grass for a bit, as if it were the smoothest polished wood floor.

She had never felt as safe as she did in his arms. She closed her eyes in confidence, knowing that he would guide her and not let her fall while *Smoke Gets in your Eyes*, played.

She opened her eyes and saw he was watching her. "Do you have smoke in your eyes now, Sparrow?"

"No. I just. I don't know what to say. Somehow, I want to say I'm sorry, but that seems small and patronizing."

"It's not."

He pulled her a little closer. The warmth of his hand on the small of her back made her stand up straighter. It was the same feeling she got when she was teaching the history of her people. It made her feel strong, loved, just as she did now. She looked up at him. It didn't seem possible. This man had been so prickly with her. He wasn't that at all. He was a nice man who had some rough spots in his life and was now facing the roughest spot of all. The least she could do was to be kind to him. So she sang under her breath the words she knew so well. "They asked me how I knew. My whole love was true."

He began singing along with her. His deep bass resonated in her. He had a very nice voice. She told him so.

"I've never heard that before."

"Well, now you have."

The darkness fell and lightening bugs enveloped them. Those in the gazebo started to dish out ice cream and serve it to the crowd. "I see they are giving out the ice cream. Do you want some?"

He shook his head. "No. I don't want any. Thank you."

His voice came low and quiet in her ear and sent a chill off inside of her. She was trying her best to protect her heart, but this proximity to him coupled with the fact they were talking to one another didn't help.

"Ok," she breathed out.

The song ended and they, as the only couple on the grassy dance floor, came off. JC was holding her hand in his and it felt so natural. So right.

They arranged themselves on opposite sides of the blanket where Carole sat with Sparrow's sisters. They were preparing to watch the fireworks, knowing full well that they both had just experienced some fireworks within.

♩♩♩

The summer camp kept going like a well-oiled machine. JC helped in so many ways. There were Tuesdays when he volunteered to help get the music together for the pageant. He joined in the sing-alongs. Some of the kids started to call him Coach because he helped with the outdoor games and athletic portion of the school on Thursdays.

He stayed late to help Sparrow clean up. One day, he asked her if she wanted to go to a movie that night.

"A movie? In town?"

"Sure. We can drive up to Atlanta. Take Carole to the drive in."

"Which one? Not Rosemary's Baby?" She made a teasing reference to the summer's biggest hit.

JC made a face. "No, I was thinking more along the lines of Sidney Poitier's new movie."

"Oh," Sparrow said.

"What's wrong with him?"

"He's alright. I mean, he's so square."

"Square? Listen to you! I thought you were interested in different perceptions of Blackness. He portrays that."

"The movies he made last year, he was at the behest of the white man. Not so great."

"Not even in The Heat of the Night when he smacked that white man?"

"Oh. Well, that was something."

"I read that wasn't even scripted. Come on. I hear the one he's in is really good. Something about Ivy."

"Oh, I did hear about that. Abby Lincoln is in it. She sings jazz and is pretty amazing. It's good to see a singer stretching her wings like that."

"Well then, it's settled. I will come by for you after dinner. We can make a bed for Carole in the back and she can go down whenever she wants."

"Sounds like a plan."

♩♩♩

"The drive-in?" Faitha asked.

"Whooo," Ronald or Donald said, making kissing noises. "Coach getting his groove going with my sister."

Sparrow chased the offending twin with a dishtowel, cracking him in the hindquarters with a sharp towel smack. "Get yourself on and make yourselves useful."

"You could leave Carole here with me." Faitha wiped her hands on another dish towel.

"I know. But thank you."

"You don't want to be alone with him."

"Not necessarily."

"What is wrong with you?"

"Mama, he's going to Vietnam at the end of the summer." The painful words echoed in her brain.

"All the more reason."

"Carole is coming. I wouldn't want to exclude her."

"Ok then. Play it your way."

"This isn't a game."

"No, it isn't. So be careful, baby girl. I have seen the way he looks at you. All those big plans you were talking about at the beginning of the summer, just might have to change."

Sparrow could see the prospect delighted Faitha, but a chill went through her. She shook it off. Her mother didn't know what she was talking about. She was mean spirited enough to have something to say. Sparrow wasn't about that. She was about having a good time.

When JC picked her up, she brought along a bag of treats with her. "We won't have to pay good money at the snack bar," Sparrow informed him and JC laughed.

"That was very thoughtful of you, Miss Jones. I could afford a bowl of popcorn."

"Well, you just might still have to buy one anyway. I love popcorn."

The drive-in was a place of great fun because there was a playground in the front for Carole to swing in and run around in so that she might get tired in time for the movie. She went in her pajamas and the disparity between wearing her pajamas in public and running around in them made her all excited. When dusk fell, they returned to the car to watch the movie.

It was a very good love story. Sparrow thought it was wonderful that Abbey Lincoln got to portray a real life human being. "She's very good in it. I think it's a new time in movies. Most times we play maids; we don't have our own lives."

Her words struck her. She must have looked strange because JC asked her what was wrong.

"I just realized what I said. The movie could be about my mother in a way."

"Is she waiting for her own Jack Parks to come along and drive her away from being a maid?"

"In a sense. I haven't been very kind to her about what she does. I mean, she does as she must in order to support us. She apologized to me. I really should apologize to her."

"Do you all not get along?"

"No. We never have. I think she blames me for ruining her life."

"You couldn't help it."

"No. But I still feel responsible."

He put a hand over hers. It was nice of him to do. By way of comfort, Sparrow let his hand rest on hers. It was a little awkward when it was time for her to go back in the house.

"Thank you for the movie. And the snacks. It was great."

"It was."

"Was this a date?"

"I believe it was," JC responded quickly and they kind of chuckled to themselves, not wanting to wake a sleeping Carole in the back of his station wagon.

"Well then, you deserve a kiss."

Sparrow leaned in to him and kissed JC on the cheek. He turned ever so slightly and captured her lips with his. A surge of surprise went through her. She really shouldn't have been surprised. She had been kissed before. But those kisses never felt like this.

His kiss tasted of home. Love. Permanence. And no music school.

She pulled back from him and stepped out of the car quickly, suddenly needing to put distance between him and her dangerous thoughts.

CHAPTER NINE

Mrs. Lincoln gave birth to a lovely baby boy the next week. Sparrow stayed away from any extra time with JC by saying she had to help get Mrs. Lincoln's home ready for when she got out of the hospital. Clearly, he was confused by why she didn't seem to want to have anything to do with him after they went to the drive-in.

Still, there were other things coming along. Like, she received the letter and tuition bill from music school in Atlanta. That bill made everything seem more real and she had to focus on that. She figured she could do music school and teach music lessons outside of class time to help support her. She would have to live at home still, but it was better than not going.

Until she got the news from the church that they would only be able to pay her $400.00 for her time as leader. They would be able to pay her the rest in the Spring. That was good news for the spring, but she needed that other $100.00 now. Her prospects for music school seemed sunk.

Still, she tried to consider the fact that JC was going to a foreign country and he might lose his life for no earthly reason. All of it, the unfairness of life made her angry. Her mother, of course, offered her the prospect of day work on the weekends. She could pull down extra for holidays. It's not what she envisioned, but after seeing For Love of Ivy, she had a changed perspective on what it meant to be a maid. Her mother certainly offered her a perspective on maintaining her dignity after what had happened to her.

When she looked down on small Robert Lincoln in his mother's arms, she did think about what it would have been like to be a young woman Beatrix's age without means or hope, finding out that she was going to have a baby.... a baby that had been forced on her.

Some force inside of her felt like sap was boiling up and she didn't know how to deal with it.

When church was over for the day, JC came to her directly. "Have you been avoiding me?"

"No. Why?"

"It seemed that way. I didn't know. We've both been so busy. I wanted to ask you to come with me to get some lunch or something."

She opened her mouth, but then shut it. There wasn't anything she could say, but yes.

"I've made arrangements with Beatrix and Candy to watch Carole."

"I hope you are paying them," Sparrow joked.

"I am."

He escorted her out of the building to his station wagon and Carole stood with Sparrow's sisters waving, calling out that she would see her soon.

Once she slid into the car, after JC opened the door for her, they started off. "What's wrong, Sparrow?"

"What do you mean?"

"I mean, I have to tell you that you've done so much to help us this summer. The last few weeks, you've seemed a bit off your game and if I can help you, I owe that to you and Carole. Aren't we friends?"

Sparrow nodded her head, tears blurring her vision. "I'm afraid I won't be able to go to school. If I don't go now, I'll end up like my mother, doing day work and with a baby, hating my children for their existence. I don't want that."

"No, that seems awful."

Sparrow sniffed, hating that her emotions were so on the surface. "The church cut my salary. I will have to do day work on the weekends at least."

"Why do you want to go to music school?"

When she was young, Sparrow wanted her voice to be ready to sing for JFK and then for Bobby. Now that he was also gone, she wanted to be ready to sing for the president, any president but LBJ. She was glad he wasn't running next year. She was mad at him for sending JC into the heart of the battle and leaving Carole to possibly be an orphan.

"I want to bring music to other people. Maybe be a teacher."

"You would be a good one. You don't want to be famous?"

"No. I had a dream to sing for the president when Kennedy was in the White House. But with this country still killing people, I don't want that anymore. I don't want to get my hopes up anymore and have them be crushed."

"This is not a great time in our country's history. I want to tell you to keep hope going, but things must look bleak. Do you have the prospect of asking anyone for a loan?"

"You mean go to a bank? What bank would give a young Negro woman that kind of money?"

She had him there. "Well, I'm going to think about this. There has got to be a solution. Meanwhile, we are going to go to a nice place and have a nice meal. And I want you to relax, Sparrow. You're doing great things with this pageant. It's going to come together and be great."

She breathed out to relax as he said, "It's going to be Ralph Bunche week. Certainly, he's a different kind of hero."

When he asked her to tell him more about Ralph Bunche, she was able to convey her understanding of his role as a broker of peace and a diplomat. She envisioned that the activities this week would take on a more international flair.

Just getting away from her environment and talking helped her a great deal. JC provided a kind of sounding board that she needed in her life. In just that minute, she was glad that it was July. She hoped September would take a long time to arrive, for both of them.

♩♩♩

It broke JC's heart to see Sparrow suffering. Her sad face was imprinted on his heart. Then, one day, it occurred him that there was something he might be able to do to help her. When the idea came to him, JC had to tamp down on the joy he felt at the prospect of being able to help Sparrow avoid what she dreaded doing in her life. But he had to think of just the right way to tell her his plan. And then, she might not accept him. Or she might want to do something else.

No. She would. She would like what he said. More and more, he was learning to pray. He took a moment there, just as he was dishing up pudding into cups for snack time to stop scooping and prayed to have Sparrow's heart hear his request. Then he kept on scooping because that might not hurt his chances either.

The next Sunday, which was the first Sunday in August, JC took Sparrow to a special place. They got in the car and he took a nice drive on the country roads in the counties south of Atlanta. Then, when he thought all was clear, he drove back to his house.

"Well, we didn't go anywhere."

"Yes. We are. Welcome to Chez St. Clair."

"Here?" Sparrow sat in the car, not taking his hand to get out.

"Yes here. I made lunch."

"Well, I have to see this."

"Don't you trust my skills? After I've been cooking at camp all these weeks?"

"You've been preparing snacks. That's not quite the same thing."

"This way, madam." He took her by the hand and helped her from the car, shutting the door carefully after her.

"What did you make?"

"I know how to make a few things."

"I've seen your house, is it...?"

"Is it?"

He could tell Sparrow was shocked to see the effort he put into cleaning the house and getting it to look in a certain way. "Yes, I cleaned it. Just for you."

"You really did. It looks great. Almost like the Claiborne house again."

"I'm glad that you like it in here."

"You do?"

"I do. Have a seat." He pulled out a chair for her at the now-cleared off dining room table.

He opened the oven and pulled out a pot roast to test it for temperature. It was starting to get cold, so he put it back in the oven to warm up. "It will take a little time for the roast and vegetables to heat up."

"It's a hot day." Sparrow took out her church program and started to fan herself with it.

"How about some lemonade?"

"Yes, please."

He chipped off some ice, put it in a glass and poured some of his lemonade on top. That was something he knew how to do very well, and was pleased to see the look of pleasure cross her face at drinking the concoction. "Do you like it?"

"It's perfect. Thank you. So, thank you for having me here, in your home."

"I should have done it before. Carole and I have been to your mother's often enough."

"It's ok. I mean, it's not my house, but I do pay her to live there. So. It's my place too."

"That's what I wanted to talk with you about. When you were talking to me about your school troubles last week, I wondered if there wasn't something I could do to help you with your schooling and something you could do to help me."

Sparrow made a face. "What would that be?"

"Well, I have to go soon. I just thought that you could be here, taking care of Carole, I will pay you to do that. It would give me great reassurance to know that Carole was in her own home. I have done enough living in other people's homes over my life. You could live here with her and you could go to school while she was in school. If you have the occasional late class, then your sisters can help. What do you think?"

Sparrow looked stunned. She sipped her lemonade. "You don't think that would be a bit controversial?"

"I don't really care what other people think. I just want my daughter to be safe and well cared for. I don't trust her with my family. I trust you. You need help with your schooling. I can give you that help. What do you say?"

"Well, do you mind if I think about it?"

"Sure. When do you think you can give me an answer?"

"After the pageant. I can't really think about anything until it's over."

JC nodded. "Sure. That's fine."

It wasn't the answer he hoped for. And there was a disappointment on her face that he couldn't quite read. "I think the roast is ready."

"Sure."

He served her roast with carrots and potatoes and they ate in silence.

"Did I say something wrong, Sparrow? I wanted to help you. I thought this plan might work."

"The way that you were going about it, I wondered if you wanted something else."

Something hit him in his gut, and he wasn't sure if he should be offended or sorry. Or both. "I'm sorry if I offended you."

Sparrow put her fork down, with only half of her roast eaten. "I'm flattered. Really. I want to help you take care of Carole. But I don't know if I should be involved in your life like that without any kind of return."

"I'm going to pay for your schooling."

"If you left Carole with me and we had no ties with one another, I could be sued by your relatives for kidnapping. She's not a puppy. Things would have to be legal."

"Well, I can ask a lawyer about that."

"Or a judge. Or Reverend Parrish."

Now he understood. "You thought I was going to marry you?"

"I guess the idea seems really outrageous." Sparrow stood.

He couldn't keep his thoughts straight. "I don't know if I want to marry again."

"Oh, I see."

"I mean you are very special to me, Sparrow, but my first wife...I mean things didn't go well. I don't want to expose myself to that again."

Sparrow stepped out from behind the table, picked up her white patent leather purse and headed for the door. "I understand. I think you might ask your family to take care of her. They're are her family, too."

"I'm not that close to them."

"Well, then you'll figure it all out. I'll see myself out."

The silence between them felt oppressive. How could he have messed everything up?

"Sparrow, I don't want you to be mad."

"Too late."

She strode quickly down his walkway with purpose and down the street.

He made the biggest mistake of his life, but he had no clue what had just happened.

CHAPTER TEN

Only the walk home served to calm her down enough to not be angry when she got to her mother's house. Sparrow didn't want to alarm Carole either.

Maybe she was more like Faitha than she thought. The thought was enough to terrify her.

Did she really want to be married to John St. Clair? She didn't really know. It would have been nice to have heard him say so. Mrs. Sparrow St. Clair had a nice ring to it, but he wasn't hearing the same ring she supposed. Still, she shouldn't have been surprised. Men wanted someone to be at home. They didn't want a woman who aspired to do things. She was still young and she thought that he understood that, given that he was pinned down when he was young. Oh. Maybe this was his way of sparing her that.

A flush rose in her hands, even though it was August. Wasn't that for her to decide? How dare he try to determine the course of her life?

By the time, she got to her mother's ramshackle house, with her brothers torturing each other on the lawn, she felt somewhat better. And slightly embarrassed.

"Where's Coach?" Donald asked.

"Mind your own business," Sparrow told him and went inside to where Carole hugged her.

"Did Daddy talk to you, Sparrow? About keeping me?"

Faitha rounded the corner and looked at both in astonishment.

"We did. And we have some more talking to do about it, honey. Why don't you go play outside for a bit?"

Carole's head lowered. "Ok."

Children knew when they were being dismissed. Her mother turned to her. "What is that girl talking about?"

"Mr. St. Clair asked me to take care of Carole while he's in Vietnam and he would pay for my schooling."

"What? Why?"

"He doesn't have anyone else to take care of her. I love her like she's my own."

"But you only 18 and you need some support to take care of a child. He didn't ask you to marry him?"

"No, ma'am."

"Well, that would have been the thing to do. That's your protection. I thought he had better sense."

"Mama, please."

"No. He better get on with that foolishness. You can get your schooling on your own. You don't need him paying for you and you have the responsibility of a child. You would be in the same position I was at your age."

Her mother had a point. Still, something about all of this left a bad taste in her mouth.

She went out on the porch to get Carole to take her back to her father's house, but Ronald told her the little girl was gone.

Sparrow started down the street in her pumps, and she saw Carole taking the path home by herself. She followed the child and saw she went up the steps to the old Claiborne house in safety.

Sparrow turned, took the pumps off her sore feet and walked back to her mother's house, wondering how in the world she would face them both the next day.

♩♩♩

Fortunately, or unfortunately, the next few weeks were crowded with getting ready for the big pageant. There were rehearsals of the play, which Sparrow had written, and of the songs. When Friday came, there was a barbecue at Second Mission with hot dogs, hamburgers and strawberry shortcake. After everyone ate, people positioned themselves in the church yard. They decided to have the performance outside to accommodate everyone that wanted to come.

Everything went off perfectly. She was proud of everyone and all their contributions. Carole stood next to her as the applause washed over her. JC came up to her with a bouquet of red roses and handed them to her. He held up a hand.

"I just wanted to thank everyone who came to see this wonderful play of faith, religion, and family. Sparrow Jones has done a wonderful job and it shows with all the children here. Now, I want to say something. I've seen her work hard. She provided snacks for the children. She worked on their costumes without asking. She poured her heart and soul into this program. Yet, Reverend Parrish said that the church would have to cut her salary by 20%. She was going to use that money to go to music school in the fall. Without it, she will have to work extra hours on the weekends. Now, as a parent and a volunteer, I think that she put in plenty of work this summer already."

He handed a hat to Carole. "My daughter, whom Sparrow got to speak after she was silent for a year and half, is coming around with a basket for donations. Please give so that Sparrow can go to school and learn even more about making wonderful music for our community, our heritage and our faith."

Sparrow stepped forward and slipped her hand into JC's hand. "Thank you. Thank you so much."

He leaned down and whispered, "I didn't want to do anything that would hurt your feelings. I hope you take this love offering and that you are successful with it."

"What about Carole?"

He squeezed her hand. "I will figure it out."

Sparrow squeezed his back. "I want to take care of her. Make it happen."

"Do you mean that?"

"Yes, I do."

He reached down and touched his lips to hers and Sparrow and JC didn't hear all the extra applause at their performance. The love offering raised was about $320.00, which would help Sparrow both terms.

♩♩♩

When JC left for Vietnam in September, he was seen onto the bottle green army plane with his daughter and fiancée wearing a wooden bangle on her arm with the Andrika symbol of Sankofa etched on it. The symbol meant that he was coming back and it showed his respect for their mutual African heritage. He also had given her a sparkly diamond on her finger showing his respect for the American tradition as well. He had arranged guardianship with an attorney and made arrangements for all of his insurances to be put into a trust in Carole's name. Just in case anything happened.

But when Sparrow touched her lips to his before he entered the jet way, he knew that was not the end for them. He would be back. There would be a future with this woman. Her kiss had just given him all the strength that he needed to return.

She would sing for him again.

Epilogue

Lark leaned over to her. "Mama. Carole is here."

Sparrow reached up and reached out for the daughter of her heart. Carole was far from the little girl who had first come to her in desperation, but she still saw something in her eyes that reminded her of the vulnerability of the small child who didn't speak.

"I'm here, Mama Sparrow. I love you."

"I love you too, daughter. I just wanted to see you one more time before I go on to glory."

Carole leaned down. "Oh, Mama." She kissed her.

"Thank you, child. Now you get that tambourine up and get to shaking it. I want to sing with these two one more time. We going to sing my song. I want you all to sing it strong. No more crying. Understand?"

"Yes, Mama." Lark came to her side.

"I hear you, Grandma," Dove echoed.

"Good. One two three..."

Sparrow tried. She tried hard. Her previously beautiful voice came out as a growl, low and hard, nothing like the voice she would use to bring people into God's arms.

She tried again, "I sing because I'm happy. I sing because I'm free. His eye is on the sparrow."

A deep voice joined in with her. "And I know he watches me."

"Chuck," Sparrow said, "You always did have a nice voice. You should have sung with me more often."

"I'm singing now, aren't I?"

"You are, my husband. Better late than never."

"I'm perfectly content to sing Sparrow's song for the rest of time."

Her loved ones saw her response in the form of a big smile on her face as she slipped into the arms of her man.

For all eternity.

PIPER HUGULEY
A CHAMPION'S HEART
BORN TO WIN MEN

Lark's Lyrics

by

Deborah Fletcher Mello

CHAPTER ONE

Lark St. Clair Warren stood in the doorway of her mother's bedroom, tears streaming down her face. Sparrow St. Clair was gone from them, death slipping in to steal her away. Losing the matriarch had broken her heart and left her shattered. She couldn't begin to fathom how she'd ever be able to get over the loss of her mother. She took a deep inhale of air, trying to stall the quiver of nerves that threatened to consume her. It felt like she'd been standing there since forever, still clutching a large mug of coffee that had long gone cold.

The subtlest breeze suddenly billowed through the space, the scent of her mother's favorite perfume teasing her nostrils. Lark clutched her free hand to her chest, new tears brimming behind her thick lashes. Unable to move herself into the room she turned, then came to an abrupt halt, spying her only child at the end of the hallway staring at her.

Dove Warren eyed her mother intently. Her expression was a wave of confusion, frustration, and hurt. She stood twisting her hands together anxiously, her eyes wide. Dove had been blessed with her grandmother's eyes and that same brilliant smile. The young woman was the spitting image of the matriarch, and for a split second the eerie resemblance left Lark slightly unsettled. She took a deep breath, and then another, to calm the wave of emotion that rippled in the pit of her stomach.

"Dove! You scared me! I didn't know you were here."

Her daughter shrugged her narrow shoulders. "I told Daddy I might stop by. It's not a problem, is it?"

"Of course, not! Don't be silly, baby girl. This is your home."

"I thought you might still be mad at me."

Lark heaved another deep breath, remembering the argument that had sent her daughter storming from their home. Since Dove had been twelve-years-old, the two had gone from being the best of buddies to constantly bumping heads. Lark swore they'd taken their mother-daughter angst to a whole other level where Sparrow had been the buffer who kept peace between them; Sparrow was now gone. And Dove was hiding out at her cousin Brenda's apartment, determined to prove she didn't need her mother for anything.

Parental advice had been the last thing Dove had been looking for when she'd come to her to share her plans for the future, plans about her career and how she thought she should reach her dreams. But advice was what she'd gotten, not wanting to hear her mother's opinion about what she should have been doing instead of supporting what she wanted to do. The harsh words they'd exchanged seemed like a lifetime ago and Lark knew from history with her own mother that it was probably just the beginning of a very bumpy road they still had to travel.

"I was never mad at you, Dove."

"Yes, you were."

"No, I just didn't agree with your decision to not compete in the gospel competition with the choir. I don't understand why you would throw that opportunity away."

"You don't want to understand. You just want me to do what you say and you don't care about what I want or how I feel."

Lark took another of the many deep breaths that always seemed necessary lately when the two were in the same room. Lark held the warm air in her lungs briefly then blew it softly past her full lips. "We're not going to fight, Dove. Not now. Please."

Contrition furrowed the young woman's brow. "Sorry, Mommy," she said, her voice a loud whisper. "I didn't mean...well...I didn't..."

Lark held up her hand, understanding washing over her.

The young woman moved in her direction, closing the space between them. She peered past her mother's shoulder into the empty room. Emotion swept between them, memories flooding both their spirits. "I miss Grandma," Dove whispered, tears misting her dark eyes.

Lark nodded. "So do I," she whispered back. She reached for Dove's hand, squeezing the young woman's fingers gently.

Lark closed her eyes, and for a moment, she remembered the warmth of her mother's hand clutching hers that very last time. The three women had been together in those final moments, linked palm to palm. Singing *His Eye is on the Sparrow*, her mother's favorite song, their melodious tones had filled the house. The walls had echoed with the weak sound of Sparrow's voice, the mellow blend of Lark's, and Dove's soul wrenching vibrato. In that moment, nothing had mattered but the love between them.

She pulled her daughter's hand to her lips and kissed the back of the girl's fingers. "Come back upstairs," she said. "I made lemon pound cake."

"You haven't made pound cake in ages," Dove said.

Her mother nodded. "I cook when I'm sad," she said softly.

Dove followed behind her mother as the two moved upstairs into the kitchen. Her father stood at the counter, filling a ceramic mug with hot coffee from the Keurig dispenser. The rich aroma permeated through the room, tap dancing with the warm scent of sugar and lemon that radiated from the sweet confection that had come out of the oven just an hour earlier.

Martin Warren looked from his wife to his daughter and back again. "We good?" he asked, a hint of concern in his tone.

Both women nodded and shrugged, a smile pulling across Lark's face. "It's still early," she said.

Dove chuckled softly. She shook her head, her eyes rolling skyward. She settled into the seat beside her father as they both stared in Lark's direction, watching as she set plates and silverware before them.

After laying out a morning feast of warm pound cake, freshly squeezed orange juice, thick hickory-smoked bacon, scrambled eggs and a mélange of fresh fruit, Lark joined them at the breakfast table.

A blanket of silence had dropped over the room, no one speaking. Words seemed unnecessary as they each fell into their own thoughts. It was one of the first times since Sparrow's funeral that they'd been able to hear themselves think. For days, family and friends had filed in and out of the home and now everyone had gone back to their routines. Despite her best efforts, Lark felt lost, desperately trying to make sense of what might lie ahead for them. She blew a soft sigh that drew her daughter's attention.

"How do you do it?" Dove suddenly asked, dropping her fork to her plate and her hands into her lap. "I feel like someone's stomping on my chest. It hurts to breath every time I think about Grandma being gone. You've gone back to being little Susie homemaker, baking cakes and acting like nothing's wrong. So how do you do it? How do you make it stop hurting?"

Lark lifted her gaze to meet the look her daughter was giving her. Her stare shifted toward her husband's. He was eyeing her back, concern washing across his expression. She turned her attention back toward Dove.

"It never stops hurting, Dove. It will still hurt years from now. You never really get over losing someone you love."

"It's not fair. I still need Grandma!"

"We may never understand why God takes people from us when he does, Dovely," her father said, calling the young woman by his nickname for her. "We just have to trust His will."

Dove tossed him a look, her gaze narrowed. "*His will*? What kind of God would...?" She bit back the rancor that suddenly pulled at her tongue, not wanting the argument she knew would come if she spoke what was really on her mind.

Lark heaved a heavy sigh. "I know how you feel, Dove. I was just about your age when my father died. When it happened, I couldn't understand why God would take him from us when we still needed him. When I still needed him. But I honestly believe that my father dying changed the trajectory of my life. I was headed downhill before that and then I met your father, fell in love, and God blessed us with you." Lark smiled at her husband, her eyes misting ever so slightly. "It still hurts, but great joy came from that pain."

Dove shook her head, a moment of confusion washing over her expression. "But you two just met in church. What was painful about that?"

The two women exchanged a look as Lark reflected on her daughter's question. There was much about her life that she had never shared with the young woman and not because she had anything to hide, but because there had never been a moment that ever felt right. Timing had never served them well.

Martin seemed to read his wife's mind. "Why don't you two make yourselves comfortable in the other room. I can do the dishes while you talk."

"Honey, no, I can do the dishes..." Lark started.

He shook his head, giving his wife a bright smile. "Go talk to your daughter," he said, his tone commanding. He leaned to kiss her cheek, squeezing her shoulder with a warm hand. "She's a big girl. She can handle it."

Lark hesitated. It wasn't Dove handling things that worried her. She couldn't help but wonder if spilling all her truth was a good thing for her to do.

Dove met her mother's gaze. "Please?"

With a nod of her head, Lark rose from her seat. "We'll be in the spare bedroom. I need to show her the box."

♩♩♩

Lark and her daughter sat lotus-style in the center of the bed that adorned the home's guest bedroom. She had retrieved a large wooden box from the top shelf in the closet and it rested on the chenille bedspread between them. Dove brushed her fingers against the carved lid, drawing a line in the faintest layer of dust that decorated the hinged top.

"I remember this!" Dove exclaimed. "You yelled at me once when I found it under your bed and tried to open it."

"I shouldn't have yelled. You were just being curious. My father made this box for me when I was a little girl. Over the years, I've kept all my keepsakes inside," Lark said as she inserted a small gold key into the lock and opened it. She rested the key against the bedding as she lifted the lid.

Dove's eyes widened with anticipation and for the briefest moment she felt herself holding her breath as Lark reached inside and pulled a black and white photo from inside. It was a picture of Lark and her father, the image torn meticulously from its other half.

Lark laughed as she passed it to her daughter. "I was angry with mother and I ripped it in half and threw the picture of her away. She and I lost so much time together because I was mad at her. For too many years I was always mad at her." A tear rolled down the older woman's cheek. "I don't want us to make the same mistakes, Dove."

Dove's eyes widened, the hurt on her mother's face pulling at her own pain. She was desperate to change the subject and lighten the mood. "Tell me about you and Daddy. Because I know you two have secrets. They started to come out at Grandma Sparrow's funeral," she said with a soft giggle. "That is until you shut them down." The young woman gave her mother a bright smile. "Tell me everything!"

Nodding her head, Lark shifted her body around and settled back against the mountain of pillows. As Dove curled up against her, extending her legs outward, Lark dropped into reflection, her words coming with the memories and the treasures hidden away in that box.

CHAPTER TWO

Lark St. Clair tossed from side to side against the padded mattress of her king-sized bed. It had been a long night at the nightclub where she performed weekly and although she was exhausted, sleep eluded her. Something felt amiss and she couldn't put her finger on what or who had her stomach twisted in a tight knot. She heaved a deep sigh as she thought about calling her mother, changing her mind before the idea gained full form.

Calling Sparrow St. Clair would surely ruin her evening, her mother chastising her yet again about something she wasn't doing right with her life. Singing secular music topped that list and Lark didn't want to hear one more lecture about her preference for R&B and not gospel.

She suddenly regretted not pursuing the honey-colored body builder she'd met earlier at the fitness center. The dark stranger might have been a nice diversion from the muddled thoughts filling her head. She was suddenly reminded of the last diversion she'd toyed with trying to forget her problems. That stranger had performed like the losing prize fighter in the eighth round of a Las Vegas title bout. Lark had hardly been impressed with his performance as he'd mauled her body with heavy hands and a bruising touch. Him not being well endowed had only exacerbated his lackluster love-making. The young woman couldn't help but roll her eyes toward the back of her head, her gaze rising to stare at the ceiling as she thought back to that moment when she'd stopped him mid-stroke and tossed him out of her bed. She laughed out loud.

Rising from the bed, she shook her head from side to side, twisting the kinks that had knotted through the muscles across her back and shoulders. She'd performed two sets that night, the room filled to capacity for both performances. She'd sung her heart out, giving the performance of a lifetime. Again. Like she did every night. Like she'd been doing since she'd been a little girl, singing in church. As she moved in the direction of the bathroom, chuckling softly to herself, her telephone rang.

Sauntering back to the bedside, Lark waited for the answering machine to pick up the call. The voice on the other end pulled at her attention, the familiar tone calling her name.

"Lark! Lark! Girl, are you there?" Carole St. Clair questioned. "Pick up the phone!"

Reaching for the handset, Lark felt herself grinning into the receiver. Carole wasn't only her family but also her closest friend. They had the same father and Lark's mother Sparrow had been the only mother Carole had ever known. Older by a few years, Carole had also been a surrogate parent as much as she'd been her big sister. Lark loved the woman with every fiber of her being. "Sissy! Is that you? What's up?

Her older sister's voice lacked her usual exuberance. "Yeah, Lark, it's me. What are you doing?"

Lark looked around the space that was her bedroom. The meticulous décor easily rivaled anything out of House Beautiful, the coordinated aqua and brown colors blending beautifully. She had chosen the colors for their relaxing ambiance. Whatever was suddenly twisting in her midsection was everything but relaxing. Lark sighed again. "Carole, please say you called to tell me something good. Please!"

On the other end, Carole shook her head hard, the phone tapping against the side of her face as she fought back tears. "I can't do that, Lark. I've got some bad news."

Lark closed her eyes tightly, leaning her head back against her neck. "I don't want any bad news, Carole. Not...now," she hissed, her voice dropping to a husky whisper.

The other woman nodded into the receiver. She paused for a brief second before finally blurting out what she had to say. "Daddy's gone, Lark. He had a heart attack and there was nothing they could do for him. You need to come home."

Lark's eyes suddenly popped open, her knees beginning to quiver uncontrollably. Swirling an about face she dropped down onto the silk chaise that adorned the far corner of the room. "What? *How*?" Lark questioned, her high-pitched tone coming too sharp for comfort.

Carole paused again before answering the question. "His heart just finally gave out, sister. He was..." Carole stalled, choking as she felt herself beginning to lose her own composure. She cleared her throat and continued. "You just need to come home. Mama Sparrow really needs you now, Lark."

Lark stammered, shock flooding through her spirit as she tried to comprehend what her sister was trying to tell her. There had to be some mistake. John Charles St. Clair was surely home, sitting in front of the late-night news espousing the state of politics in America, and Noah Wyle and Eriq LaSalle's performances on the last episode of ER. Carole had to be wrong. "No...he can't...it's a lie...Mama...can't....no, no, no, no, no!"

"I'm so sorry, Lark. I hate that you had to hear it like this. I'm going to send someone to get you. He's a friend from the church. You really need to come home and I can't leave Mama to come get you myself."

"No, no, no, no, no...."

Always the calm and controlled older sister, Carole continued. "His name's Martin. You might remember him from the neighborhood. Mama Sparrow says you two used to play together when you were little. He'll call you, Lark. Just be ready when he gets there, please."

Carole was still holding the receiver as her baby sister's screams echoed over the phone line.

♩♩♩

Lark was still wailing when Martin Warren pulled into her driveway, some three hundred and fifty miles from his own front door. Her screams had stalled to a low sob. When the request had come from Carole and Sparrow St. Clair, Martin hadn't hesitated, jumping at the chance to be of service. He'd called the young woman to say he was on his way and neither of them had disconnected the call. Martin had driven with his flip phone pressed to his ear, his battery about to need a serious resuscitation. He had murmured softly into the receiver as Lark had bemoaned the tragedy that had befallen her beloved father. Martin felt that it had only been right for him to hold on for as long as he had. He owed Sparrow St. Clair that much and maybe even a bit more.

Lark was lying naked on the floor of her bedroom when Martin used the key hidden in a flower pot to enter her Baltimore, Maryland home. He felt just uncomfortable enough to be nervous, like he was intruding where he didn't belong. Carole had forewarned him about Lark's state of mind when she'd told him where to find the secreted key. The words "emotional" and "dramatic" suddenly echoed in his head.

Climbing the stairs to find her, he could smell her signature cologne, a lavender and vanilla musk, before he saw her. The fragrance was spirited and teasing. Her body was curled around an oversized pillow, the satin pillow case damp from her tears.

Kneeling beside her, Martin called her name, drawing his large hand against her hip and thigh. The sensation of her warm skin against his cool palm sent a chill up his spine. He shook the feeling from his head, snatching his hand from her as if he'd been burned.

"Lark, it's me, Martin. I'm right here. Please, don't cry any more. Everything's going to be okay," he said, his other hand caressing the length of her hair as he instinctively drew her into his arms and held her close.

Lark's sobs rose once again as she let her tears fall against Martin's chest. "Why?" she cried, the mournful wail filling the man with anxiety. "Why? Why did this happen to my daddy? This can't be right!"

Martin shook his head, knowing that he didn't have an answer that would bring her any comfort. "I don't know, Lark. We just have to accept that it's God's will."

Lark snapped upright. What kind of God would take such a phenomenal husband and father from his family? She didn't bother to voice the thought aloud. She wasn't interested in the theology she was sure

Martin would spout to rationalize her father's passing. There was absolutely nothing right about her father dying. Nothing. She turned to stare, fully looking at him for the first time.

As if a light bulb had been turned on, recognition suddenly swept through her. Martin Warren from Miss Hamman's fourth grade class was in her bedroom. Martin Warren who'd been her lab partner at John R. Griffin Middle School had just hugged her. Martin Warren who'd often followed her home to eat in her mother's kitchen, had teased her about wearing a bra, and had told the Parrish twins she was a horrible kisser was seeing her at her most vulnerable.

Of course, she remembered him from the neighborhood. He'd been her first crush and her last love. Mostly, he'd been her best friend until the day he hadn't, life sending them both in different directions. Back then, everyone had called him Sugar, because of the juvenile diabetes that had required daily doses of insulin to be injected into any area of fatty tissue his grandmother had been able to find on his frail body.

"Boy got 'sugah'," the old woman had uttered the first-time Lark had watched him be injected, her eyes widened in awe.

"Sugar's blood is too sweet," his father had echoed, a hearty chuckle resounding through the room.

As Lark thought about it, she couldn't remember if she'd ever known his government name. He'd been Sugar when they were nine and he'd been Sugar when they turned nineteen. Clearly, knowing their history, her sister Carole had jokes and Lark didn't find anything about it funny.

She heaved a deep sigh, suddenly self-conscious about her nakedness. She pushed him from her as she reached for the cotton sheet that had fallen from the bed, tucking it tightly around her body. Her gaze locked with his, the man barely blinking an eye.

Martin Warren seemed completely unfazed by the situation they found themselves in. "What do you want to do?" he asked, knowing her answer before she uttered it.

As she moved to rise, he helped her to her feet, his gaze following behind her as she moved into the bathroom and the shower, her bare backside seeming to beckon his attention. He couldn't help but appreciate how she moved with an unconscious gracefulness. Every step she made served to seduce him into senselessness and he was certain that was not her intent.

He closed his eyes, his teeth clenched as he fought the swell of emotion sweeping through him. Reminded himself why he was there in the first place. Feeling as if he'd disrespected her father's memory, guilt and then contrition, flooded his spirit.

"I need to get back to North Carolina," Lark said, her words echoing through the room. "I need to be with my family."

CHAPTER THREE

Two hours later Lark had packed enough clothes for a year-long trip and had secured her home as though she had no plans on returning. After a quick stop to drop her cat off at a neighbor's, they were navigating I-95, headed back to Fayetteville, North Carolina. Martin reached for the cup of Dunkin Donuts coffee that rested in the center console, sipping the hot fluid carefully. Beside him, Lark had fallen into a fitful sleep, finally allowing herself to rest. He knew she wouldn't sleep long but he was glad to see her relax if only for the moment.

Stealing sidelong glances at her, Martin couldn't help but be completely intrigued. Lark St. Clair had been having that effect on him since they'd been little kids doing nothing more than contemplating dryer lint as they sat on the steps of his family's home. Back then the old folks had called what he felt for Lark puppy love. He couldn't help but wonder what they might call it today.

Her head was cradled comfortably against the headrest; her eyes closed easily, her mouth opened ever so slightly. The glossy black curls of her hair framed her perfect oval-shaped face, falling to brush against her shoulders. There was nothing to her, the petite woman barely a hand full. Even in the four-inch heels on her feet she barely came up to his shoulder.

Martin had been amazed at how small she had felt in his arms, his thick limbs easily wrapping around her.

Her skin was the color of rich, dark chocolate, glistening like something rare and expensive. Martin imagined that she might taste as delectable. Sneaking another glance, he inhaled swiftly, then blew warm breath past his full lips as he fought the urge to draw his fingers along the line of her cheek.

The woman was even more beautiful than he remembered and he remembered everything about Lark. How could anyone forget the way she could always wrangle him to do things he had no business doing? Her makeshift singing group, Lark and Crew, had been the beginning. Martin could feel himself smiling as he thought back to the motley group of military brats from the base housing complex on Fort Bragg that had rounded out their circle.

Lark had been their superstar and every superstar had a best friend. Patricia Louise Brown had been Lark's. Patricia had been as plain as a brown paper bag, wearing Coke-bottle glasses that covered her crossed eyes and a bad stutter when she got nervous. Her saving grace had been the lithe body that moved with the grace of a gazelle on the African plains. Patricia could out dance them all and her choreographed moves were supposed to have set Lark and Crew far above and beyond the rest. Lark had nicknamed her Brown, simply because she was.

Cassius Perry had lived in the house next door to Martin, moving from Fort Campbell to Ft. Bragg the summer they both turned ten. The boy had been Hershey's chocolate dark with a fondness for the sweet confection. With his robust frame, gregarious personality, and delectable complexion, Lark had called him Chocolate for his obsession with the delight.

Last, but not least, was Joseph Wagner. Joseph had been the oldest of them all. At thirteen, he'd stood as tall as some men twice his age. Joseph had a swagger that had made the young girls giggle and whisper with appreciation. He also had his own guitar, with all the strings. Lark nicknamed him Strings for just that reason.

Lark's half-sister Carole had been added to the group by default. Admonished by Mama Sparrow to not let the little girl out of her sight, Carole had picked up a tambourine, positioned herself just close enough to feel included and called herself a backup singer while she spent most of her time with her head in a book.

Like most of them, Martin had been born into the military, in Germany, where his father had been stationed. Before Ft. Bragg he'd moved five times. There had been four schools, an array of houses he barely remembered, many friends, and a multitude of tears. Lark had been lucky. Ft. Bragg had been her father's last installation. It had been the only military base she'd ever known.

Their makeshift band had been a nice diversion for all of them, giving them something else to focus on besides the constant deployments of friends and family. Sitting out on those steps, humming up lyrics and following Lark's directives had kept them out of trouble for a short while. That is until Lark had found trouble, leading them all astray instead.

Lark had deemed herself their leader in charge, proclaiming that her pleasant disposition made her the best choice for the job. But there had been nothing pleasant about Lark St. Clair and no one had had the courage to tell her so. No one... but Martin. From day one Martin had told her nothing but the truth. Doing so had put them at odds more times than not. But there had been no time when Lark hadn't been able to trust what Martin had to say to her. They'd found friendship, claiming something precious between them and even now, returning to where it all began, both instinctively knew they could trust each other.

Too much had happened to the two of them over the years. Fate had dealt them different hands. Martin had chosen to stay in North Carolina, dedicating himself to the church they'd been raised in and the students he mentored in his position as a music professor at Fayetteville State University. Lark had left him and Fayetteville behind, determined that no one and nothing would ever hold her hostage there. She'd gone searching out a music career, determined to sing her songs, her way. Now she was headed back, the home of the airborne whispering loudly for her return.

The young woman shifted in her seat, her dark eyes opening widely, a bad dream startling her from her sleep. Her gaze shifted toward Martin, his attention diverted as he stared out to the highway, his focus fixed on getting them back safely.

She sat upright and looked around. "Where are we?"

"We're close. We should be there in an hour or so," he said, his own eyes moving to the digital clock on the dashboard.

Lark folded her arms over her chest, her hand pulling at the seat belt strap that had tightened across her breasts. She leaned her head against the passenger side window. "Why haven't you ever called me, Sugar?" she suddenly asked, breaking the silence that spun like thick mist through the space. "And who named you Martin?"

♩♩♩

Martin Warren was beautiful, a perfect blend of European and African roots. Lark stared at him intently as his hazel eyes danced between his mirrors and the roadway ahead of them. She had always loved to stare into his eyes, to lose herself in the heat they always seemed to exude. Every time Martin looked at her, it was as if his stare was a raging fire ready to ignite a spark deep within her. Now, with everything that had happened in the last few hours all she wanted was to linger in the heat of him, where she felt safest. A faint smile pulled at her thin lips.

Martin was almost too pretty for his own good, she thought, her head lightly waving from side to side. His build was solid, the man clearly treating his body well. There was no ignoring the broad shoulders, massive pecs, and thick muscular legs of his large frame beneath the stark, white dress shirt and gray slacks he wore. His complexion was the color of rich caramel, the hue like no one else's she knew. The taut skin, molded over rock hard muscle begged to be touched. Lark resisted the urge to do just that, clenching her fists tightly in the pockets of the jacket she wore.

She inhaled swiftly. She couldn't remember a time when being with Martin didn't take her breath away. Even as a little girl, when she'd gone out of her way to try to be mean to him, the nearness of him had kept her off guard. She hadn't realized just how much she'd missed him until she'd heard the deep vibrato of his voice bouncing off her bedroom walls and now the nearness of him was taking her breath away.

Her gaze met his just as he reached his large hand out toward her, resting it lightly against her forearm.

"Are you okay?" he asked softly, his gaze shifting from her face to the road and back.

Lark shook her head, tears pressing hot against the back of her eyelids. "No."

"How long has it been since you were last home?"

"When did I leave?" she answered, hating to admit that it had been a few years since she'd last visited. She'd sworn when she'd gotten on the bus, headed out of North Carolina, that nothing was ever going to bring her back. But here she was, knee deep in the Carolina Sandhills once again.

An hour later Martin pulled his car into a designated parking spot in the lot of Second Missionary Baptist Church. There was a parking spot sign that read Choir Director, situated between the spaces labeled Pastor and Deacon. Lark peered out the window, staring first toward the signs, the old brick church building, and then back at Martin. She cast a questioning eye in the man's direction.

"Your mother told me to bring you here before heading to the house. She said she'd be waiting for you," Martin answered, his deep voice soothing. "Are you ready for this?"

They both knew she wasn't ready so she didn't bother to respond. Instead she sat in wait as Martin exited the car, moving around the front of the vehicle to the passenger-side door. Reaching for the doorknob, he opened it and extended his hand to help her out. A shiver of energy raced up the length of her arm as Martin entwined her fingers with his. He squeezed her hand gently and Lark allowed herself to squeeze back. Even under the circumstances, it felt good to her to be back home; returning feeling less daunting. Martin's presence had her at ease and the sensation was disconcerting, throwing her for an unexpected loop. She took a deep breath to shake the feeling.

As the duo stepped through the church doors Lark was suddenly nervous. The last time she and Martin had been together, they'd been here in the sanctuary, alone, arguing about Lark wanting to leave. Nothing he'd been able to say had been enough to convince her to stay. Everything he hadn't been able to say had left his heart, and hers, broken. Lark had walked away and had never looked back.

Sparrow St. Clair sat in the front pew, her head bowed in prayer. Lark could feel her mother pleading, every silent word begging God for solace. She rushed forward, moving swiftly to the woman's side. She threw her arms around her mother's shoulders.

"Lark! Lark!" the older woman gushed as she planted a wet kiss against Lark's cheek. "My sweet songbird! You came home!"

Tears spilled like rain out of Lark's eyes. "Oh, Mother! I'm so sorry!"

The matriarch gripped Lark's face between her warm hands. "It's going to be okay. Your daddy loved you very much, Lark. I hope you know that."

Lark nodded. "I know. But it's just not fair."

Sparrow smiled. "My Chuck's in a better place. I'm sure your daddy is up there giving everyone a hard time."

"Making them do pushups, I bet!"

Sparrow laughed. "He only made you do pushups, little girl! Had to keep you in line somehow."

Lark's warm laughter rang through the sanctuary with her mother's. The two fell into a quiet reverie, whispering quietly together. Martin stood off to the side, his hands laced together in front of him, his stance at attention. He waited patiently for their cues. He found himself thinking back to the days when all was well between them; Lark and Crew had reigned supreme, Lark and her mother had been the best of friends and Lark's mother made the best macaroni and cheese in the neighborhood. Life had been simple and they had all been happy. He couldn't help but wonder when it all had changed. Sparrow interrupted his thoughts.

"Martin, I need to run over to Sister Russell's to drop off the obituary for the program. If you would please lock up the church and then take Lark home I would really appreciate it."

She turned to her daughter. "The funeral is the day after tomorrow and I want you to sing for your father, Lark."

Lark's eyes widened. She stammered, "I can't…I don't…"

"Your father would probably like I Go To The Rock. He always loved it when you sang that song. He used to brag that you put everyone else to shame when you sang it. Then maybe we we'll do a duet together. I think Really Gonna Miss You would be good. What do you think, Martin?"

"Whatever you want, Miss Sparrow," he said softly.

"I don't think…" Lark started.

Her mother held up her hand, stalling her words. "It'll be fine. It'll be a going home that will make your daddy proud. You'll do fine." Sparrow leaned to give her daughter one last kiss on the cheek before she continued. "Martin will help us make sure everything is perfect."

Sparrow tossed Martin a slight smile. "Your daddy always did like that young man," she said to Lark, her voice dropping to a low whisper meant only for Lark's ears. She gave the young woman a quick wink, tossed her hand up in a slight wave and eased down the aisle and out of the church.

Lark's gaze shifted toward Martin. "She never asks what I want. Just orders and demands and insists."

"You've always been an obedient daughter. Miss Sparrow trusts you'll do what's right."

Lark laughed. "I don't know how obedient I was. I left, remember?"

Martin chuckled. "You had moments."

"What if I didn't want to sing at my father's funeral?"

"You don't want to?"

"I haven't sung in church since I left Fayetteville."

"It's like riding a bike," Martin said with a wide smile. "Once you step up there it'll feel like old times."

Lark rolled her eyes. "So why are you here again?"

He chuckled. "I'm the choir director here at Second Baptist."

Her eyebrows lifted in surprise. "Mother made you, didn't she?"

He laughed. "Your mother can be very persuasive and when the position became open, it just felt right."

Lark paused a moment to ponder his comment. If she were honest, she couldn't remember what it felt like for things to feel right. It had been a long time since anything in her life had felt right. She suddenly felt a little jealous.

Martin interrupted her thoughts, his deep voice intruding on the quiet that billowed through the rafters. "I should get you home. Your mother will be looking for you."

"And I'm sure your wife is probably expecting you back about now, too."

He shook his head. "No wife. No kids."

"I would have thought you'd be married by now."

"Still waiting for the right woman."

"That might be a long wait. My mother says none of us are perfect."

"Your mother also says that we shouldn't strive for perfection. We should strive to be our best. That's why I'm waiting for the right woman, not the perfect woman." His expression was smug as he eyed her.

Lark chuckled softly as she stared back at him, amusement dancing across her face.

He extended a hand in her direction. "Are you ready, Lark?"

She hesitated, her eyes skating to the baby grand piano. "Do you still play, Martin?"

He nodded. "I do."

"Play for me," she said as she moved up the short flight of steps to the altar.

Martin nodded as he followed behind her. He settled himself on the piano bench, allowing his fingers to skate the length of the keys and back. The first round of chords brought tears to Lark's eyes but she came in right on key, the first bars of Up Where We Belong echoing through the sanctuary. As he joined her in the chorus, she was reminded of how nicely he sang. There was a maturity to his tone that she found compelling, one that hadn't been there the last time they'd sung together. They ended the evening with a rendition of I Don't Know Much before Martin closed the lid to the piano and stood up. "I missed you, Lark," he said softly.

Lark smiled. "I'm sure you did!"

CHAPTER FOUR

The day John Charles St. Clair was laid to rest, friends and family witnessed a musical ministry unlike anything they had ever experienced before. His wife and daughter poured every ounce of hurt and pain they were feeling into the service and the songs they sang to honor the patriarch's memory. Folks had been on their feet in praise and worship, awed by the powerful presence that seemed to possess the two women.

Days later, Lark was trying to determine when she would return home, ready to leave Fayetteville behind. Her family wasn't happy about her wanting to go.

"You should come home and stay," Carole admonished. "Mama Sparrow needs you here."

Lark cradled Carole's baby girl against her shoulder. The little bundle of joy slept peacefully in her auntie's arms, oblivious to the family drama playing out around her.

"I have a life in Baltimore and I like it there."

"But singing at that night club hasn't gotten you anywhere," Sparrow said, interrupting the conversation. "You're wasting your gift, Lark. God blessed you with a beautiful voice and you should honor him by using it. You know I always...."

"...wanted to sing for the President of the United States!" Lark echoed in unison, having heard the tale at least a billion times.

Carole laughed. "You two need to stop."

"Well, that was my dream," Sparrow snapped. She reached to take the baby from Lark's arms.

"But it wasn't my dream, Mother."

Sparrow's gaze locked with Lark's. "No, it wasn't, was it."

Lark had been singing before she learned how to walk. As an infant, she'd cooed in tune with her mother whenever Sparrow sang. She'd been two, maybe three the first time her mother had let her sing in church, knowing all the words to This Little Light of Mine. By the time she was twelve-years-old, the two were singing a duet at every Sunday service. Known as the St. Clair Belles, there had been guest appearances at other churches, gospel competitions and a host of performances that still made Lark cringe to remember them. Sparrow had proclaimed her daughter the next Shirley Caesar and Lark aspired to be the next Mariah Carey or Whitney Houston.

Her senior year in high school Lark and her mother had barely spoken unless it was to argue about where and what Lark would be singing next. Sparrow had become the stage mom from hell and by graduation, Lark had had enough.

On her eighteenth birthday, she'd packed a bag, written a quick note, and had caught the first bus leaving North Carolina. It had stopped in Maryland and so had she, eager to do her life her way.

The two women were still staring at each other when the doorbell suddenly rang, interrupting the moment.

"That would be Martin," Sparrow quipped. "I asked him to come by. Thought you might like to get out of the house for a minute."

Lark blinked rapidly, her lashes like little fans. Carole giggled at her from the other side of the room. Lark snapped, "Are you serious, Mother? You arranged a date for me?"

Sparrow shrugged. "I asked a family friend to stop by the house for a minute. I thought he could show you around town since it's been a long while since you've been here. If you want to call it a date that's on you."

Lark shot her sister a look. "Did you know about this?"

Carole shrugged. "I am not in this. You two will need to work this out all on your own." She moved from the kitchen to the foyer and opened the door.

Lark could hear Martin's deep voice vibrating through the space as he greeted her sister warmly.

Sparrow grinned as she nuzzled her nose into the soft folds of her granddaughter's neck. "More than one way to skin a cat! Ain't that right, Brenda? Grandma loves her baby!"

Lark shook her head. She looked like she might combust when Martin suddenly appeared in the doorway.

"Good afternoon, Miss Sparrow. Hey, Lark! How are you ladies today?"

"We're good, Martin! How are you, dear?"

"I'm doing well, thank you. Is everything okay? You said it was urgent that I stop by."

Sparrow nodded. "I need you to get Lark out of the house. She's going stir crazy and needs a break from her old mother. You have some time, don't you, dear? Lark was just about to run upstairs to change her clothes. She should be ready in a quick minute. Isn't that right, Lark?"

Lark's mouth dropped open as she snapped to attention. She tossed Martin a look, laughter dancing across his face as he eyed the St. Clair women with amusement.

Carole grabbed her arm and pulled her from her chair. "She'll be right back," her sister chimed as the two exited the room and headed up the stairs. Under her breath, she muttered, "Don't say it! I know what you're thinking!"

"I'm thinking our mother has lost her mind," Lark snapped.

"That may be true, but don't you say it."

"And you want me to stay around for more of this?'

"I want you to stay because it will be good for her. And for you."

Lark shook her head. "You're crazy, too."

Carole laughed. "It runs in the family. So, you'll think about it?"

Lark gave her sister a look. "Maybe."

"I'll take that."

♩♩♩

Martin maneuvered his car toward Haymount, the downtown area of Fayetteville. Lark had barely spoken two words to him, still peeved by her mother's antics. Notorious for her tantrums and mood swings, Lark sitting quietly was quite the change and it had Martin slightly unnerved. He cut an eye in her direction as he took a left turn past the Bragg Boulevard entrance to the military base.

"Do you want to talk about it?" he asked.

Lark peered over her sunshades. "Do you always do everything my mother tells you to do?"

"Yes," he answered matter-of-factly. "There's nothing I won't do for your mother. Miss Sparrow is a pretty special lady and she's been really good to me."

"She's not that special," Lark muttered.

Martin chuckled. "Your mother helped me get through some tough times. She was there for me when my grandmother passed and when my father died. I don't know that I could have gotten through without her support."

"Your father died?"

He nodded. "The year after you left."

"I'm so sorry. I didn't know," Lark said, suddenly feeling like the worst friend in the world.

Martin shrugged his broad shoulders. "It's all good. I'm glad we have this opportunity to catch up with each other. And I'm grateful that your mother helped make that happen."

Lark cut an eye in his direction. "I guess she's good for something," she said, a smug smile pulling at her full lips.

He laughed heartily.

Minutes later the two were seated on the patio of Huske Hardware House. The restaurant and brewery was one of Martin's favorite spots to kick back. He'd ordered wings and chili fries for them to share and two craft beers. Lark felt herself relax for the first time since leaving Baltimore.

"So, you like teaching?" Lark questioned, taking a sip of her brew.

"I do. I enjoy it very much. But I like the work I do at the church more."

"The choir is very good. I was very impressed."

"Thank you. We work very hard."

"I actually miss singing in the church choir."

"You don't have a home church in Baltimore?"

Lark shook her head. "No. After I left here, I was determined to never step foot in anyone's church ever again."

"How's that working out for you?"

Lark smiled. "Don't tell my mother, but it wasn't one of my brighter decisions."

"You always did do things just to be spiteful."

She shrugged. "I'm getting better. I think."

Martin laughed. "So, tell me about your life. What's been going on with you since you left?"

Lark blew a heavy sigh, reflecting on the choices she'd made since turning her back on everything she'd known. Baltimore hadn't been in her plans, the stop meant to be a stepping stone to bigger and better. Needing to put money in her pockets, she'd landed a waitressing job at the small nightclub where she now performed six nights out of seven. Maneuvering her way on stage had come with much effort and a lot of luck. Becoming a headliner was supposed to bring in a record deal and make her a pop star. But Lark was still waiting for that spotlight to shine. Sharing all of it with Martin left her feeling slightly vulnerable.

He shifted forward in his seat. "So why are you still there, Lark? If it's not what you really want, why are you wasting your time?"

She blew a soft sigh. "Honestly? In the beginning, I did want it. I truly believed I could be a superstar. The club's manager introduced me to some industry professionals and I thought it would all work out. After a while though I realized the only reason I wanted it was because my mother's been telling me that I should since I was a little girl. But now," she shrugged, "not so much."

"So, it sounds like you have some decisions to make."

Lark nodded. "I guess I do."

Their conversation continued for another good hour. The mood was light and easy, both comfortable as they became reacquainted. Martin stole a quick glance down to his wristwatch.

"Are you in a hurry to get back home?"

Lark shook her head. "Not at all. What are you thinking."

Rising from his seat, he tossed two twenty-dollar bills onto the table to cover their tab. "My dance class starts in thirty minutes."

Lark's eyebrows rose curiously. "Dance class?"

He grinned as he reached for her hand and pulled her along. "Do you salsa?"

♩♩♩

The ride took them across town to Baile con Sazon dance studios. There was a nice crowd gathered and everyone was in a good mood. The Caribbean rhythms vibrating out of the large, black speakers made Lark smile and in no time at all she was having a great time as Martin led her across the dance floor, spinning her left and then right as he guided her in the basic salsa dance steps. Hips shifted, shoulders rolled and the two were soon giddy with joy as they moved in perfect sync with each other.

Lark tossed her head back against her shoulders, enjoying the music as it vibrated through her body. Martin grinned as he watched her. Lark was the life of the party and there was no missing the many eyes on her. She had caught the attention of all the men and most of the women and she relished the interest. Her carefree spirit felt right in a way he had never understood before and he was savoring every minute of her company.

"You're really good at this!" Lark exclaimed as he spun her in a circle and pulled her back to him. His large hands rested easily against her as he pushed and pulled her into position.

"You're not so bad yourself," Martin answered as her body lightly grazed his own, the heat between them rising with a vengeance.

Lark's smile was wide as her hips rotated seductively from side to side, the easy gyrations pulling at his attention. Martin bit down against his lower lip to stall the quiver of heat that pulsed through his lower quadrant. He took a deep breath and then a second. When the class finally ended, neither of them was ready for the night to end.

Standing in the parking lot, Lark moved herself against him, pressing her palms to his chest. Her body followed as she moved in closer. Her expression was coquettish and teasing. "So, maybe we should take this party to your place," she whispered huskily.

Martin smiled, his brow raised. "I think that we should...."

"...go make sweet, sweet love to each other," Lark said, interrupting his comment.

He shook his head. "I was going to say we should get you home. I'm sure your mother is expecting you."

Lark tossed her arms around his neck. "My mother can wait," she said as she rose up on her toes, moving to plant a kiss on his lips. She bristled when he suddenly turned his head, purposely avoiding her touch.

She took a step back, her eyes wide with bewilderment. There was no missing the incredulous expression that crossed her face. Lark had never known any man to turn her down. Martin was the first to ever refuse her advances. She was suddenly feeling some kind of way.

"Please, take me home," she snapped, her arms crossing over her chest.

Martin took a deep inhale of air. "Don't be mad, Lark."

"Who said I'm mad? I'm not mad. I just want to go home," she answered, her curt tone resonating with venom.

Martin chuckled, his head waving from side to side as he studied her intently. Kissing Lark had been on his mind since he'd walked into her mother's home. He used to dream about kissing Lark. Fantasizing about making love to her had gotten him through many long, lonely nights. Any other time he would have welcomed her advances, jumping at the opportunity to be close to her. But this wasn't the time.

He reached for her, dropping a warm hand against her forearm. "You are mad. But you'd be angrier if I allowed something to happen when you're not ready."

"Obviously, I must be ready," she retorted. "Or I wouldn't have extended the invitation."

He shook his head. "Your father just died, Lark. You need some time to get over that. You shouldn't be making any major decisions for at least six months. And extending invitations into your bed is a major decision."

"It was just sex, Martin. I wasn't asking you to marry me."

"No," he said, shaking his head ever so slightly. "It would be much more than just sex for me. And that's another reason why we shouldn't rush into anything. I don't plan to let you break my heart a second time."

"A second time? I didn't..."

He interrupted her. "Yes, you did. When you left, you hurt my heart, Lark. It took me a minute to get over that."

She shook her head. "I don't understand."

"Do you remember the argument we had that last time, before you left town?"

Lark shrugged. "You told me not to go. That's what I remember."

"I did. What I didn't say was that I wanted you to stay because I wanted more than just friendship. I wanted us to see where we could take our relationship. I was in love with you, Lark."

"But you never said anything!"

"Because you weren't in love with me. You wanted bright lights and your name on a billboard. You were self-absorbed and only focused on your singing career. I couldn't compete with that so I didn't try. I let you go and I eventually got over you leaving."

"But I did love you," Lark snapped back, the words coming before she could catch them. Her eyes widened, the confession tinting her cheeks a deep shade of embarrassed. Her heart was racing and her breath caught deep in her chest.

Energy shifted in the late-night air. Something neither could explain seemed to pass between them. Above their heads a full moon loomed bright and full. Lark stared at him, her eyes dancing over his face. He seemed to be studying her closely, light shimmering in his dark eyes. He was smiling at her, the upward curl of his lips dimpling deep wells in his cheeks. There was something about the look he was giving her that suddenly pulled at her heartstrings.

"I'm sorry, Martin...I didn't know...I didn't..."

Martin reached out and drew his index finger along the profile of her face. He took a step forward, his large frame looming above her. Wrapping his arms around her torso, he pulled her close and kissed the top of her head. "Your mother is probably starting to wonder where you are," he said softly. "So, I need to get you home."

♩ ♩ ♩

"Am I self-absorbed?" Lark asked, lifting her eyes to stare at her sister.

Carole stared back, the question giving her reason to pause. "You have moments."

She blew a soft sigh. "Martin said I hurt him when I left."

"You hurt all of us, Lark."

Lark dropped her gaze to the floor, counting the square tiles that ran the length of the room. In the distance, she could hear her mother humming softly to herself, chiming in with the music that flowed from the stereo. Sparrow had been spinning love songs for most of the afternoon; Thinking of You by Sister Sledge, Barry White's Can't Get Enough of Your Love, Babe, Donna Summer and Love to Love You, Baby. One after another, syncopated stories of love lost, and love found, and love that was true, and good, and necessary, and sometimes sexy, dirty, and downright nasty.

Lark allowed herself to fall into the moment, thinking about her parents, and Martin, and the space she suddenly found herself in. Anita Baker and Sweet Love pulled her to her feet and into the room where her mother sat singing along.

Sparrow smiled, gesturing for Lark to turn down the volume on the music system. "What's wrong, songbird? You look like you lost your best friend?"

"I feel like I did," Lark said, Martin still in the forefront of her thoughts.

Sparrow chuckled softly. "Martin's not going anywhere, songbird. As long as you give him hope he'll be right here waiting for you."

"You knew?

"How he felt about you? Everybody knew."

"I didn't.

Her mother narrowed her gaze. "You knew. You might not have said it out loud but you knew. And you took advantage of it every chance you could."

Lark didn't bother to respond. Instead, she moved back to the stereo and turned the volume back up. She moved to the window to stare out over the landscape. In the background, Peaches and Herb were singing Reunited.

CHAPTER FIVE

Martin wasn't expecting Lark to call so when she did, it actually surprised him. "Hello?"

"Sugar, hey. It's me."

"Lark?"

"Were you expecting someone else?"

"No. But I wasn't expecting you either."

"Ouch!"

He laughed. "What's up?"

"I was wondering if you might be available for dinner?"

"Tonight?"

"Yes, tonight. They're having an open mike night down at Chiefs," she said. "I thought it might be fun to just hang out."

"With me?"

"Well, I'm not calling anyone else, am I?"

There was a moment of pause as he considered her request. "I think that's doable," he finally said.

Lark giggled. "Are you making this difficult on purpose?"

"No, I'm really just surprised. First, that you called and second that you're inviting me somewhere."

"Well, don't be. So, are you available?"

He smiled. "I'll be there with bells on."

Chiefs was a little hole in the wall juke joint that played the hottest music and had really great wings and ribs. It catered to a twenty-five and up crowd and guaranteed its patrons a good time. By the time their food arrived, Lark and Martin were bantering back and forth like old times, both enjoying each other's company. Laughter was abundant as he teased and she teased back. They fell into an easy rhythm with each other and there was a level of comfort that both had missed.

"I've decided to stay here in Fayetteville," Lark said as she swiped her hands across a paper napkin. "I was hoping you'd give me a ride back to Baltimore to get the rest of my things."

Martin smiled. "I'm sure your mother is really happy about that."

"Are you happy that I'm staying?" Lark asked. She shifted forward in her seat.

His expression was smug as he pushed his shoulders toward the ceiling in an exaggerated shrug. "Maybe."

"Maybe?"

"I might be feeling some way about it."

Lark laughed. "You're funny, Martin Warren. Very funny."

He laughed with her. "I'm happy if it's going to make you happy, Lark. But what about your career?"

A low gust of air blew past her lips. "I really don't want to sing anymore. At least not in the clubs."

"How is Miss Sparrow going to feel about that?"

"I don't know. But I have to do what feels right for me."

Martin nodded. "So, what do you want for your life, Lark?"

She met his gaze with one of her own. A slight smile pulled at her mouth, showcasing picture perfect teeth. "For now, I just want to take things one day at a time. I can't make any life changing decisions for a few more months, remember?"

Martin nodded and then he reached for her hand, pulling her to her feet to spin her on the dance floor.

♩♩♩

When Lark showed up for Thursday night choir practice, Martin couldn't stop grinning. She took a seat in the back row, nervous tension teasing her spirit. The other members had welcomed her warmly, delighted to have Sparrow St. Clair's daughter join them. Rhonda Bishop was the only one who eyed her warily, already sensing the demise of the few solo numbers she'd been previously afforded.

Martin immediately put them all at ease with laughter, cracking one bad joke too many. Once the last stragglers arrived, the few cell phones in the room were silenced and everyone was in place, he warmed them up with some vocal exercises and simple breathing work. Singing tongue twisters seemed silly at first but Lark welcomed the results, feeling completely at ease by the time he moved them into more serious work. It was musical therapy in its purest form and owning how much she'd missed it was eye-opening.

By the end of practice, they'd prepared two songs for Sunday service, both led by Mr. William Hyatt, one of her geriatric favorites and a longtime friend of Lark's late father. The old man's deep baritone was perfect for his rendition of Sam Cooke's Touch the Hem of His Garment. And despite his reservations, Martin had convinced the old-timer to do the Mighty Clouds of Joy's Walk Around Heaven. When the evening was over, Lark was excited about being a part of the group and discovering where she would eventually fit into the dynamics of what they all brought to the table.

She stood at the piano as Martin walked Rhonda down the aisle. The young woman's dress was just short enough to be too short and form-fitting to the point of being too tight. She looked like she was headed to the club and the four-inch love me pumps weren't helping. Lark didn't miss the look the woman was giving her favorite choir director, her intentions everything but Christian-like.

She slid her hand across the piano, the tinkling of the keys drawing Martin's attention. Rhonda frowned, clearly not amused as he turned from her to stare where Lark sat at the piano bench. Lark began to play, the soft tune billowing through the sanctuary. She began to sing a soulful rendition of Hallelujah, filling the room with the beauty of her voice. The moment was captivating.

As Lark finished, Martin was still staring. Looking defeated, Rhonda turned toward the door. With a wave of her hand, Lark wished the woman a good night. "See you Sunday!" she exclaimed, the eagerness in her voice moving Martin to laugh.

He moved back down the aisle to join her. "That was..." he started.

"Intentional," she concluded, her brow raised. "Sorry, but I didn't like how she was looking at you."

Martin laughed. "I was going to say that your performance was beautiful. But how was Miss Bishop looking at me that you needed to do that on purpose?"

"Like she wanted you to dip your biscuit in her gravy. She needed to be reminded that she was in church."

He shook his head. "That is not how..."

"It was. Trust me. I know."

Martin reached for her hand and entwined his fingers between hers. He changed the subject. "So, when do you want to head to Baltimore?"

"It'll be a week or so. I need to put some things in place and the club wants me to give one last performance while I'm there. Once I leave, I don't want to have to go back."

"Just let me know, please, so I can arrange my schedule."

Lark nodded. "So, while, we're having this discussion, what's the deal with you and Rhonda?"

Martin shook his head. "There is no deal. She and I are just friends."

Lark stood up, gesturing toward the exit. "Let's lock up and you can tell me all about it over dinner."

He laughed heartily. "But there's nothing to tell."

"Uh huh."

"Honestly!"

"I'll be the judge of that."

"You have some nerve," Martin teased as they made their way down the aisle.

Lark smiled. "I'm just catching up on everything you've been into since I've been gone!"

♩♩♩

The trip to Baltimore came a few weeks later. Martin and Lark had driven up early in the morning to meet her landlord who wasn't overly excited about losing a tenant. After packing the last of her personal possessions into the back of his SUV, the two had gone down to the harbor to enjoy lunch and a quiet moment together.

The bonds of their friendship had grown exponentially. The two spent hours talking about everything and about nothing. Lark allowed herself to be vulnerable with Martin in a way she had never been vulnerable with any man. He shared secrets with her that no one else was privy to. She learned that he still favored fried bologna sandwiches and he teased her about her obsession with mint chocolate chip ice cream. She laughed at his jokes and he feigned interest when she gossiped about people she knew. They'd revived a childhood friendship and allowed it to mature into something uniquely special. Something that was becoming increasingly important to them both.

"Are you sure about performing tonight?" Martin asked as they stared out to the water and the boats docked in the inner harbor.

Lark nodded. "I am. One last hurrah."

"It doesn't have to be. You can still pursue a music career, Lark.

"I really don't want to. For the longest time, I thought it was about the kind of music I was singing. My mother wanted me to sing gospel and I didn't want that. Now that I've been able to sing everything else, I realize I just don't want to sing. Not as a career. I love that I'm back in church and if I'm honest that's all I ever needed."

"So, what do you want, Lark? What does your future look like?"

Lark cut her eyes in his direction, then shifted her gaze back out over the harbor. "Don't laugh at me, but I really just want to be a wife and a mother. I want a family and a husband. I want what my parents had. What my mother enjoyed with my father. If I could have that, life would be golden. I wouldn't need anything else."

Martin nodded. "Do you think you could see yourself having that with me, Lark?"

Lark smiled. She shifted her body closer to his, leaning her head against his shoulder. "I can't see myself having that with anyone but you, Martin."

Tossing an arm around her shoulder, Martin pulled her even closer. He lifted her chin with his forefinger, raising her gaze to his. His eyes danced with hers, skipping across her face. A wave of heat coursed like a storm wind, spinning them both into a reverie that neither could have imagined.

Lark whispered, "Are you ever going to kiss me, Martin Warren?"

He smiled sweetly. And then he did, his mouth claiming hers possessively.

♩♩♩

The Sinner's Den was hidden away in a block of brick buildings condemned by the city. It boasted a loyal clientele, well-stocked bar, and some of the best music in the state of Maryland. The line to get into the building extended down to the corner, a crowd of well-dressed patrons anxious to get inside. The hotspot was an industry favorite, some of the music profession's elite occasionally dropping by to jam with the band. Performing there had blessed Lark with the opportunity to sing for some heavy hitters and had her heart truly been in the game, could have taken her musical career to a whole other level. For the first time, Lark was willing to admit that her heart hadn't been in it.

Lark pushed her way through the crowd, past the bouncer who greeted her warmly and into the club. Martin followed closely on her heels, everyone eyeing him curiously. He felt like her personal body guard as he gave the men who were ogling her, the evil eye. The club's owner was heavyset with a full head and beard of snow white hair. Against his dark complexion, it was stunning and from the women crowded around him, garnered him much attention. He tossed his hands up as he jumped from his seat to wrap her in a deep bear hug.

Lark hugged the man back, then turned to introduce them. "Martin Warren, this is Randolph

Cutter. Randolph, I'd like you to meet Martin Warren."

Randolph extended his hand. "It's a pleasure. So, you're the man who has stolen our songbird's heart."

Martin chuckled. "More like our songbird has stolen mine!"

The older man nodded. "Well, any friend of Lark's is a friend of mine. Make yourself at home and if there is anything I, or my staff, can get you, just ask."

"Thank you, sir! I appreciate that."

"Word's spread fast that this is your last performance here, Lark. All these people showed up to see you."

Martin didn't miss the moisture that suddenly dampenedd her gaze. Lark took a deep inhale of air as she looked around the space.

"You can still change your mind," Randolph said, his head tilting slightly toward her.

Lark shook her head. "No, it's past time, Randolph. All the while I've been gone, I didn't miss it. I didn't miss any of it so I know it's time for me to pack up and move on."

"Then go out with a bang, baby! Make sure these fools know they are going to miss you. Sing sweet for us tonight."

Lark reached up to hug the man one last time. "I'll give them a show they won't soon forget," she said softly. She brushed a kiss against the old man's cheek, then gestured for Martin to follow her to her dressing room.

Once the door was closed behind them, her tears fell, rolling like mist over the round of her cheeks.

Concern washed over Martin's expression. "Are you okay?"

Lark nodded. She stepped into his arms and pressed her face to his chest. "Just closing one door for another," she answered.

He nodded his head in understanding, holding her tightly until her anxiety fell away.

Lark took a breath, then stepped away from him. "I need to get ready," she said as she turned toward the makeup table. "Why don't you have a seat and just talk to me."

"What do you want to talk about?" Martin asked.

She smiled. "Our future."

When Randolph introduced Lark for the last time, a captivated audience gave her a standing ovation, welcoming her to the stage. Martin watched proudly as she stepped out to greet them. She smiled brightly, her hands extended before her and then she took a slight bow, bending forward from the waist. She wore a dress of silver sequins that fell to the floor and she'd pulled her curls into a messy up-do that flattered her face. She was the most beautiful woman in the room and he suddenly felt like the luckiest man in the world.

Lark sang her heart out. The repertoire of music resonated with every person watching. She and the band played off each other, the bond between them evident in the ease of each changing tune. She sang as if she never intended to sing again and the crystal clarity of her voice brought many of them to tears. The hour-long set passed by and was gone in the blink of an eye.

Lark clutched the microphone, slipping it back into the stand. She closed her eyes and stood still, the low warble of the horn joined by the trill of the piano filling the room. When she opened her eyes, she was staring directly at him. Martin sat up straighter as a spotlight suddenly shown down on him.

Her voice came low and seductive. "I'd like to dedicate this next song to a very special man. He's been my best friend and my biggest supporter and I love him with everything in me. Martin Warren, this one's for you, sugar."

"Always and forever, each moment with you..." The Heatwave song echoed through the space and pulled a smile across his dark face as he stared at her. With the last note, Lark blew him a kiss and took her last bow. The crowd cheered and few of Lark's fans slapped him against the back. And just like that, Lark St. Clair's musical aspirations were over.

CHAPTER SIX

The man standing in Lark's dressing room, met Martin's look with a sneer. He was tall and lanky, dressed in high priced sneakers, low-slung denim jeans, and an ornate gold chain around his neck. His tone was possessive as he called her name.

"Lark, so you're just going to show up and leave without saying anything to me?"

Lark stopped short, her gaze sweeping the man up one side and down the other. "Excuse me?"

"You heard me."

Martin felt himself tense, the other man's tone riling his emotions. Lark shot him a look, sensing the rise of hostility growing like a fungus around them. She dropped her hand to his, her fingers warm against his skin.

"KJ, you need to leave," she said, her monotone voice showing no emotion.

"We still have business to discuss. "

"No, we don't."

"How can you say that? We have a contract and I have to hear in the streets that you're quitting your gig here and moving back to Podunk, North Carolina."

Lark shook her head. "We do not have a contract. You don't own me and you sure as hell aren't going to tell me what I can and cannot do."

"We have a verbal agreement, Lark. I promised to take your career to the next level."

"Well, I'm no longer holding you to that, KJ. There is absolutely nothing you can do for me from this point forward."

"Baby-" He took a step toward her.

Martin bristled with indignation. "Lark, who's your friend?"

She took a deep breath. "Martin, this is Kenneth Jordan Murphy, KJ to his friends and family. KJ, this is Martin Warren."

Kenneth Jordan Murphy didn't bother to give Martin a look. "What about us, Lark? You're just going to walk away from what we had?"

Martin inhaled swiftly, air catching deep in his chest. "Maybe I should wait outside," he snapped, his eyes narrowed as he tossed Lark a look.

"That's a good idea. Why don't you go do that," KJ quipped, his voice dripping with attitude.

Lark rolled her eyes skyward, her head waving from side to side. "You should stay right where you are," she said, locking eyes with Martin. She shifted her attention back to Kenneth.

"Kenneth, I'm not sure what your problem is, but there is no us. There has been no us since your last little tryst with that lounge singer from the Caribbean. What was her name again? Brittney, Bianca, Brianne? Oh, I remember, didn't you call her Butterball? Something about that nice, tight..."

"That was a misunderstanding, Lark. There was nothing going on with me and that girl. I swear."

"Just like you swore you weren't sleeping with that backup dancer and the girl from the Dairy Queen."

"Okay, so maybe I slipped up once or twice. You're the only one I truly care about, Lark."

"I'm done, KJ. We're done. Enjoy your life. I plan to fully enjoy mine without you."

"What about our dreams? We were going to build an empire together?"

"Baby, you were going to build an empire. I was going to support your dream. I have no interest in doing that anymore. But you know this. Don't act like we've never had this conversation before."

"You owe me!

"I don't owe you anything!"

KJ suddenly grabbed her arm, pulling her to him. He slipped an arm around her waist, holding her tight. Lark pushed him from her, slapping her palms against his chest. "Get your damn hands off me, KJ!"

The man moved to grab her a second time when Martin suddenly stepped between them. He threw the only punch, nailing KJ with a fist to the side of his face. The man's head snapped as he fell backwards and dropped like lead weight to the floor. Lark's eyes were wide as she looked from one to the other. A slow smile pulled across her face.

Martin shook his hand, opening and closing his fist to move the blood through the vessels. He met the look she was giving him. "You have any other ex-boyfriends I need to know about?"

Lark shook her head. "No."

"Good. I don't think we'll be having any more problems out of this one but if he ever puts his hands on you again, I will hurt him."

Lark grinned. "Damn, that was hot!" she exclaimed.

Stepping over the man, Martin reached for her hand. "You ready?"

She nodded as she slid her palm against his. "I've never been more ready!"

♩♩♩

Martin pushed the lawn mower from one side of the yard to the other. Sparrow stood at her kitchen window and watched as he pruned the new growth of grass, each row neat and even. He paused to tuck a small towel into the rear pocket of his jeans. Lark peered over her mother's shoulder.

"How long has he been cutting your grass?"

"Years now. When it got to be too much for your father, he just showed up one day and took over. Never asked for a dime. Just volunteered his services."

"He says he owes you for everything you've done for him."

"He doesn't owe me for anything. He went through a hard time after his granny passed and then when his daddy was killed, he just needed people to care about him. All we did was show him some love."

"How was his father killed?"

"He never told you?"

"I never asked. I didn't want to upset him."

Sparrow nodded. "He was trying to stop a robbery at the Save-Mart and he was shot. It was tragic."

Lark looked back out the window. Martin had paused again to wipe the sweat from his brow. He'd taken off his shirt and was bare-chested, the midday sun shining down against his brown skin. He was a beautiful specimen of male prowess, muscles hard and rippling, and a near perfect six-pack screaming for attention. She couldn't help but wonder what his skin would feel like beneath her fingertips. She closed her eyes and imagined herself touching him, caressing each sinewy muscle, learning every dimple and scar. Her eyes snapped open as a wave of heat flowed through her feminine spirit. She took a deep inhale of air and held it, sucking in oxygen a second and then a third time to regain her composure.

"Mother?"

"Yes, songbird?"

"How did you know Daddy was the one? When you two started dating, when were you sure that he was the man you were meant to spend forever with?"

Sparrow smiled as she thought back to her husband and the beautiful relationship they'd shared. "Your father made my heart sing," she said softly. "That's when I knew. And you will too. When a man makes your heart sing then you'll know he's the one!"

Lark took a deep breath, returning her gaze to the beauty outside the window.

Her mother chuckled softly. "Right now, Martin has your heart skipping some quick beats. I'd say the band is gearing up to play you a love song. When you hear it and your hearts jumps in on the chorus, you'll know."

♩♩♩

Weeks later, Hurricane Floyd, a category four storm was predicted to hit the east coast with a vengeance. Lark and Martin carried gallons of water from his truck into her mother's home, stocking the pantry in preparation. Outside, the winds were beginning to kick up and the clouds had started to roll through. Carole sat in front of the television, updating them all with the weather predictions.

"They're saying Florida will be hit the hardest," she reported. Baby Brenda sat in her lap, gnawing on a strap from her mother's apron.

"We should still be ready," Sparrow said, as she moved from her kitchen into the living room. "You never know with these things. Anything can happen."

Lark shrugged. "We need to run some water and extra blankets down to the church.

They're using the fellowship hall to shelter anyone in need. Right now, there are ten families who plan to ride out the storm there."

Sparrow nodded. She moved to give Lark a hug. "You and Martin be safe out there, please."

Lark hugged her mother back. "We'll be fine."

"I'll take good care of her, Miss Sparrow. I promise. We're going to come right back."

The matriarch nodded. "You should plan on staying here tonight, Martin. No point in you planning to go back home alone."

"Yes, ma'am."

Everyone turned to stare at the television, listening to yet another update on the storm's potential path.

"Well, get a move on it you two," Sparrow suddenly admonished. "Those winds are picking up out there!"

♩♩♩

Martin pulled into the driveway of his home. The sky had finally opened, the beginnings of a torrential rain starting to drench everything. The single-family house was a 1930's charmer with two bedrooms, one bath, and a spacious back yard. It was simple and clean and possessed a wealth of character

"This is lovely!" Lark chimed as she took a quick tour, moving from room to room as Martin tossed a change of clothes into an overnight bag.

"It's comfortable. I haven't needed much so it's worked for me. I imagine you're going to want something a little bigger."

Lark tossed him a look. "One day. I'm sure we'll need room for all those kids you want to have. For now, though, I think it's perfect for just the two of us. It's quite cozy."

Martin laughed as she eased behind him, wrapping her arms around his waist. "You're wet, baby! How'd you get so soaked?"

"You must have missed all that rain coming down outside. I didn't have an umbrella, remember?"

He wrapped his arms around her and kissed her lips. "Oh, I remember."

"Maybe I should get out of these wet clothes and toss them into your dryer. In fact, you're wet too. Maybe we should both take off our clothes," Lark said, her voice dropping an octave as she teased him, her body gyrating a slow, seductive twirl against his. "We wouldn't want to catch a cold now, would we?"

Martin chuckled softly. "No, we definitely don't want to catch a cold."

Lark licked her lips, the sensual gesture slow and easy.

"There's a storm coming, Lark."

"Uh, huh." She pressed a kiss against his Adam's apple, trailing her tongue over the spot her lips had touched.

"I'm sure your mother is wondering where we are right about now."

"Uh huh." She undid the buttons on his shirt, her fingers gently pulling at the barest hint of chest hair. She planted another kiss between his clavicle.

Martin felt every muscle in his body quiver and then harden. He drew in a quick breath and grabbed her wrists, stalling her ministrations.

"Lark, we shouldn't..."

"But you want to."

He nodded. "I do, but..."

"No buts, Martin. You want me and I want you." She reached up to kiss his mouth, pressing her lips to his. "What are we waiting for?"

He grabbed her hands again, kissing her fingers. "Are you ready for this, Lark? I mean, really ready for what this means?"

A hint of confusion washed over her expression. "I'm not sure what you're asking me, Martin."

"I'm looking for a lifetime with you, Lark. I want you to be my wife and have my children. I want us to grow old together and when we make love, whenever that is, there will be no turning back from that. At least not for me. I need the same assurances from you. I need to know that you want forever with me as much as I want it with you."

There was a quick moment of pause.

A tear rolled down Lark's cheek. "Martin, I love you," she said softly. She wrapped her arms around his neck and drew him to her. "I have loved you since forever and I will love you till the end of eternity. And making love to you will be everything you and I will ever need or want it to be."

A wry smiled pulled at Martin's full lips, the wealth of it dancing across his face. There was a glow that flushed Lark's face and a light that shimmered in her eyes. Everything about her had him feeling as if everything was good in his small world. He captured her mouth beneath his own, kissing her hungrily. His touch was sweet and tender, a gentle brushing of flesh against flesh. His tongue snaked past the line of her lips to tangle with hers. It was a deep, tongue-entwined kiss that left them both panting in anticipation.

Lark shed her clothes like a butterfly shedding its cocoon. She did a slow, erotic striptease that incited every nerve ending in Martin's body to fire. She exposed beautiful brown skin inch by inch as she peeled off her sweatshirt and jeans, then her lace bra and panties. His eyes were wide with wonder as he stared, awed by the sheer beauty of her. She was absolutely divine and in that moment, she was all his.

Lark melted in his arms as Martin quickly stripped out of his own clothes and wrapped himself around her. She reveled in the nearness of him, his taut skin sliding like melted butter against hers. His hands danced across her pear-shaped breasts, pulling at the hardened nipples. The chocolate protrusions had him salivating for more as his tongue skated from one to the other and back.

With his lips pressed gently against her neck, Lark could smell the subtle scent of coconut milk, aloe and shea butter in his hair, the scent of his favored conditioner teasing her nostrils. The air in the room was suddenly hot and humid. He pushed her toward the king-sized bed, snatching the covers to the floor. They both fell back against the mattress, his body covering hers. Their limbs were entwined and perspiration beaded over heated skin.

His sheets were freshly washed and newly changed, the soft thread-count caressing her back and shoulders. Her body arched with pleasure as his hands slid beneath her buttocks and lifted her groin into his own. Air caught in her chest when every inch of his nakedness kissed hers, their bodies fitting nicely against each other.

"I...love...you," Lark muttered between stifled moans. "Oh...Martin...I...love..."

Martin smiled, his gaze focused, his stare a wealth of emotion. He kissed her again, no words needed to tell her that he loved her, too. He slid his tongue along the line of her ear lobe, sucking at the soft flesh. She shivered with lust and expectation, her body quivering beneath his own.

The moment was surreal, time seeming to stand still. They were locked closely together in the warmest embrace. Martin licked his right index finger and ran it slowly from her chin to her navel. Lark shuddered as he ran his hands down the inside of her quivering legs, teasing every nerve ending. In one swift movement, he slid from her torso to the well between her legs, pleasuring her with the tip of his tongue. Lark gasped, throwing back her head with a scream of sheer delight. He dropped deeper into the warmth of her most private place, his tongue sliding up and down, catching the sweet nectar that dripped in abundance.

Her first orgasm erupted with a vengeance, his mouth locked possessively around her moans. He slid back up her torso until his pelvis teased hers. He was hard, his own need urgent and then he slid himself into her, one swift motion locking them tightly together. Lark's body opened to welcome him in, her inner lining pulsing voraciously around him.

He held himself there, savoring the sensation of her touch and the softness of her body as it caressed his own hard lines. With slow and easy strokes he began to push and pull himself against her, the tempo rising with the heat between them. His body felt like it would combust as she stroked and teased him, her hands skating across his broad back and buttocks. It was ecstasy, the beauty of it beyond any words the two could muster.

Lark screamed his name and he echoed her cries with his own. The intensity of the moment wasn't lost on either of them. When he orgasmed, her body erupted with his, the rapture of their loving sending them both over the edge. As the beat of her heart synced with his, nothing else needed to be said, the commitment between them ingrained in every breath they shared.

♩♩♩

Outside, the storm was slamming the state of North Carolina. At its peak the winds hit over a hundred and forty miles per hour, upending trees, and property. Massive flooding followed, adding to the devastation from one end of the state to the other.

Inside, Sparrow was still fussing at Lark and Martin, a whole other storm brewing with a vengeance.

"You two had me worried to death! I don't know what you had to be thinking!"

Lark and Martin exchanged a look, slight smiles pulling at their lips.

He answered for them both. "I do apologize, Miss Sparrow. We didn't anticipate taking so long and I surely didn't want to worry you."

"We're safe, that's all that matters, Mother." Lark sighed.

Sparrow looked from one to the other, studying them intently. She suddenly nodded her head, a moment of understanding washing over her. She laughed lightly, her head waving. "Martin, what are your intentions with my daughter?" she questioned.

"Ma'am?"

"You heard me!"

Lark laughed. "Mother!"

"Don't mother me! You know your father would be asking him the same thing. I'm just doing my duty as your parent."

Martin grinned. "I plan to marry Lark, Miss Sparrow. I promise you I will make an honest woman out of her!"

Sparrow chuckled warmly. "And what about her career? She has a gift and she needs to..."

Lark interrupted her mother's comment. "Stop! Please! We are not having this conversation."

"But, Lark, you need to sing and you..."

"No! I need you to let me live my life my way. That's what I need. And I don't want this to be an argument with us anymore. Please, Mother! Please!"

Sparrow took a deep breath. She and her daughter stared at each other, something between them shifting abruptly. Tears misted the older woman's gaze. She turned away to stare out the window. She watched as the trees swayed from side to side looking like they might snap, but enduring, the limbs sturdy as the leaves blew about with complete abandon. She started to hum softly.

Moving to her mother's side, Lark slipped her hand into her mother's hand, interlocking their fingers together. Her tears had spilled over her cheeks, a heated drenching just shy of a full-blown sob.

Behind them Martin eased his way out of the room, the private moment meant only for the two of them. As he made his way to the kitchen, mother and daughter began to sing, the soft lull of their voices blending beautifully together, misting his own eyes with tears.

CHAPTER SEVEN

Choir practice had been over for a good few minutes. Everyone had left, headed home, leaving Lark tinkering with the piano keys. Martin moved from the church office back into the sanctuary. There was something pulling at them both, each noting that the other wasn't in usual form.

He looked around. "Did Pastor Robins come through here?"

Lark nodded. "He left. He said he would call you about the choir's visit to Mt. Moriah next week. I told him we would lock up the church as soon as you were done."

Martin nodded. He took a deep breath. "I was thinking we could grab dinner and then maybe go to my house. There's something I need to talk to you about."

"There's something I need to tell you, too," Lark said. Her gaze skated around the sanctuary, fighting not to meet his eyes.

Martin moved to where she was, dropping down onto the piano bench beside her. "Maybe we should just talk then," he said softly.

Lark cut her eyes at him. "What's wrong, Sugar?"

He shook his head. "There's nothing wrong. I was offered a job. The church we visited last month in Virginia has asked me to come head their choir."

"Virginia?"

He nodded. "They're offering a very nice salary. I also made some calls and there's a possibility that I can also teach at Virginia Commonwealth University. I'd be making enough money that you wouldn't have to work if you didn't want to. You could be a stay-at-home mom."

"Virginia?"

Martin took another deep breath. "I know you've just settled in from moving back and this would be another change, but we could make it work, Lark."

Lark dropped her eyes to the piano and played the scales up and then down. She could feel Martin staring at her, waiting for her to say something. She lifted her eyes to his, the slightest smile pulling across her face.

"I'm pregnant," she said, the pronouncement coming abruptly. "We're having a baby!"

His eyes widened in surprise, the news completely unexpected. "Are you sure?"

Lark nodded. "I am definitely sure," she said, tears suddenly rising in her eyes.

He reached for her, pulling her into a tight embrace. "Sweetheart, it's going to be okay! Don't cry! You do want this baby, don't you?"

"Of course, I do! I was scared you wouldn't be happy about the news."

Martin laughed. "The woman I love is having my baby. That's the best news I could have ever gotten!" He hugged her tightly.

"How soon would we have to move?"

"Very soon. They want me in place by the end of the month."

Lark nodded. "How would you feel about my mother moving with us?"

He looked surprised. "Your mother?"

"I can't imagine having this baby without her being there to help." She swiped at a tear that tangled in her lashes. "She might not want to leave but I would like to ask."

Martin kissed her. "I'm sure Miss Sparrow wouldn't want to miss any of this either!"

♩♩♩

Sparrow knocked on the bedroom door, pushing it open before Lark had chance to invite her in. The young woman looked up from her packing, clothes strewn all over her bed and floor.

"May I come in?"

Lark laughed. "I think you're already in, Mother!"

Sparrow stood in the center of the room. She laughed, too, as she moved to the bed and took a seat. "I promise to do better when we get to the new house."

Lark smiled. She stopped what she was doing and took the seat beside her mother. "Is everything okay?"

Sparrow nodded. "Everything is wonderful. My baby girl is getting married. I'm going to be a grandmother again. And we're all starting a new adventure in Virginia! I'm doing better than okay."

"Can I tell you something?"

Sparrow reached for her daughter's hand. "Of course, songbird! You can tell me anything."

"I'm scared. It's so much and it's happening so fast."

Her mother nodded. "It is. But you're not alone. Martin is a wonderful man! And he loves you! As long as you two are willing to work together, you'll be able to get through anything. And I'll be right there to help if you need me."

Lark laughed. "Being bossy and nosey, no doubt."

"Of course!" Sparrow gave her daughter a big hug. She blew a soft sigh as she reached into the pocket of her housecoat.

Lark's gaze fell to the wooden bangle the matriarch pulled from her pocket. It rested in her mother's palm as the woman flipped it from one hand to the other. The rosewood bracelet with its carved Adinkra symbols had been a gift from her father, one her mother treasured immensely. Sparrow only wore it on special occasions and it was usually tucked away in her jewelry box the rest of the time.

Since her father's death, her mother often sat toying with the trinket, seeming to find comfort from just having it in her hands. Lark eyed her mother curiously as the matriarch slipped the bangle onto her wrist, twisting it back and forth.

"I'm going to get out of your way, but I just wanted to come tell you I love you, songbird. You have always been my pride and joy."

"I love you, too."

"I wish your father could be here," Sparrow said, fighting not to cry. "I know he would have been as excited for you as I am," she concluded, still twisting her bracelet.

Lark wrapped her arms around her mother's shoulders and hugged her.

Minutes later, when Martin knocked, peeking into the room, the two were still holding tightly to each other, lost in conversation about the wedding, the move, and the new baby.

♩♩♩

Two weeks later, Pastor Jerome Robins pronounced Lark St. Clair and Martin Warren husband and wife. Carole stood with her sister and Sparrow gave her daughter away. The intimate ceremony was witnessed by their church family and their closest friends. The moment was more than either had ever imagined and everything they had ever fantasized.

Lark twisted the wooden bangle on her wrist, the carved detail moving her to smile. Sparrow had gifted the trinket to her as she'd been preparing to take her wedding vows. The moment had been one she would always remember. She suddenly imagined when she'd be able to give her own daughter the gift, passing it down as her mother had passed it to her.

Martin eyed her curiously. "You good?"

Lark laughed. "Your daughter just kicked me."

His eyes widened as his smile spread full across his face. "Daughter?"

"Our baby is a girl. I can feel it."

He nodded as she grabbed his hand and pressed it to her stomach. There was a light thump, thump, thump against his palm. His smiled erupted to a full grin, big and bold and filled with immense joy. "That's my baby," he said.

Lark laughed, the wealth of it filling the space between them. "That's our Dove!" she exclaimed.

Epilogue

Dove wiped a tear from her eyes. She lifted her head from her mother's lap. They'd been talking for hours, the story of her parent's courtship leading to another story and then another and another. For the first time, she felt as if she understood her mother more than she ever had before. They had laughed together and cried and she'd been overjoyed to discover her mother hadn't always been reserved and proper, sometimes breaking the rules and most times making up her own.

Lark threw her legs off the side of the bed. "I need to go check on your father. He's probably wondering what happened to us."

Dove smiled. "I hope I'll have what you and Daddy have one day. Grandma had a great love story and you, too. I hope I'll have that."

"You can have everything you want, Dove. You just have to work hard for it." Lark winked an eye at her daughter as she moved toward the door. "Do me a favor, please. Put my things back into the box. Thank you!"

Nodding, Dove reached for the photo of her mother and grandfather, flyers from the night clubs where her mother had performed and the assorted knickknacks that had marked moments in time for

Lark. She laid them carefully into the box, her mother's wooden bangle tucked into a corner.

In the distance, Dove could hear her parents laughing together. She knew her father had hugged her mother the moment she'd entered the room. The two had always been openly affectionate with each other. Growing up, their kisses and hugs were as common as sunshine and rain. Their love had filled their home and Dove trusted the abundance of it, needing it like air. The deep bass of someone's love song suddenly billowed from the other room. Dove didn't need to see them to know they were doing a slow dance in the kitchen, her mother humming along with the song in her father's ear.

Reaching for her cell phone, Dove dialed and waited for the call to be answered on the other end. "Brenda, hey, it's me. Girrrrllll, do I have some tea to tell you!"

Deborah Fletcher Mello
Wherever books are sold!
Deborah Fletcher Mello
GRAYE
DEBORAH FLETCHER MELLO

Dove's Dream

By

Iris Bolling

♫

CHAPTER ONE

"Daddy, where is she? Please tell me she isn't gone," Dove cried as she ran into the house, dropping her treasured purse to the floor.

"Dove." Her father caught her by the shoulders with love. "Your mother is with her." He held her at arms-length and looked into her tearful eyes. "She is asking for you." Dove tried to pull away, but he held her steady. "Listen to me. She is weak and her time is near. This is your chance to tell her how much you love her and to listen." He emphasized the word again. "Listen to what she has to say."

Dove heard her father's words, but she did not want to believe her life was about to change. She shook her head and was about to pull away when he stopped her again. "Dove, I know you are scared and hurting, however, please know this moment is hers. It's about her, not you, not your mother...her. Listen with your heart."

Dove pushed away from her father. She stood there staring at him with troubled eyes. "Is this your doing? Did you do this to bring me back to your precious choir?"

Her father exhaled and turned away. "No, Dove. This isn't about you." He walked away shaking his head.

Dove watched his back as he walked out of the room. There was something different in the air. She ran down the stairs, to the basement of the three-level home, she ran away from the night before. She walked swiftly through the family room, down the hallway to her grandmother's room.

Her mother was sitting beside the bed holding her grandmother's hand.

"Mother?"

Lark turned to see her rebellious daughter standing in the doorway.

"She's here," she whispered to her mother. "See," Lark said as tears streaked down her face. "I told you she would come." Lark stood, as she motioned for her daughter to come into the room. Lark was certain Dove did not want to be in the same room with her after the argument they had the night before, so she kissed her mother's cheek. "I'll be right outside the door. Promise me you will stay."

"Now, child, you know I can't control the Lord." Sparrow gave her daughter a faint smile.

"I don't believe that for one moment." Lark smiled through another teardrop. She gently placed her mother's hand on the bed, then walked over to the doorway. "I'll be outside the door if you need me." She touched her daughter's arm, then walked out.

Dove couldn't believe how frail her grandmother looked. Did she look that way yesterday? She couldn't remember.

"Nothing in here is going to bite you, child. Come talk to me."

Dove wiped the tears, then walked over, took her grandma's hand and sat beside the bed.

"When I was young I told my mother I was going to sing for the President of the United States one day." Sparrow smiled at the memory. "It never happened, but I never let the dream go. I tried to force your mother to live my dream and I was wrong. It took her walking away for me to realize it. We missed precious time. You brought us back together. There is a lot of love around you, child. You are young and just starting your journey. Learn from the lessons of mine and your mother's. Let the petty stuff go. It ain't nothing but the devil trying to keep you from all the love God has put in your path.

"We are a family filled with love. This fight for me is over, Dove, but yours is just beginning. The battle is not with your mother. It is within you. You can't fight with yourself—you'll lose every time. God gave you and your mother a gift. Don't throw it back in His face. Embrace it, your way, not mine or your mother's. That's all He asks, and you will be okay. Wipe those tears away. Don't cry for me. Sing for the life God gave me. You and your mother have always been my greatest joy. Now sing me to sleep."

Dove turned to the doorway. "Mother," she called out as she dried her tears with the backs of her hands.

Lark walked into the room. Dove held her hand out. "Let's sing for Grandma."

The three joined hands and began to sing her favorite song, *His Eye is on the Sparrow*. The melody filled the house, with the weak sound of Sparrow's voice, the mellow blend of Lark, and the booming, soul wrenching voice of Dove. When they sang together in church they were called the St. Clair Belles. Today, they were simply, grandmother, mother, and daughter.

Lark was the first to notice when Sparrow's voice trailed off. She squeezed her daughter's hand to encourage her to continue as tears streamed for the hand of the woman who gave her life, was no longer gripping, yet still warm inside hers. The link was still there, not as tight, no longer living, but there with the three generations of voices.

CHAPTER TWO

"Of course, Dove will sing," Lark said as she sat at the kitchen table writing down the plans for her mother's service. "Mother always loved her voice."

"She may not want to honor her grandmother in that way. It may be too much for her," Martin, her husband replied.

"Why not ask the question before you make yet another commitment on my part?" Dove asked as she walked into the kitchen.

"It's your grandmother's funeral. I wouldn't think I'd have to ask."

"Her body left the house less than an hour ago. Let's just take a moment to deal with your mother's death?"

"Dove," her father cautioned. "Your mother is just as upset as you are."

Dove rolled her eyes towards her mother. "Why not wait for me to offer?"

"Is it too much to ask my only child to honor her grandmother?"

"It wouldn't be if you asked. But you didn't. Like always, you just assumed I would be at your beck and call for another church performance."

"This isn't about the church," Lark shot back. "This is about my mother...my mother is dead. You can't begin to understand the grief I am experiencing because you've never lost anything in your life! "she yelled as tears streamed down her face.

Dove watched as her father gathered her mother into his arms, then held out a hand to her. After a moment's hesitation, she took it, then reached up for her mother's hand. Tears rolled down her face.

"I do feel your pain. She was your mother, but she was also my grandmother."

Martin smiled, then gathered her into his arms as well. "It's a good thing I have long arms. I can hold both of you at the same time."

Dove and her mother chuckled as they wiped tears.

Lark sighed as they all sat back down at the table. "I'm sorry, Dove. I should have asked. Will you sing for your grandmother?"

Dove nodded. "*His Eye is on the Sparrow*."

Lark smiled. "That's one of her favorites, and mine, too." She squeezed Dove's hand and nodded. "Good. Darling, you will of course handle the choir, Reverend Paul will do the eulogy, Brenda and the rest of your cousins can be flower girls."

Dove glanced up at her father as they both shook their heads. "Mother, I think you may want to ask people before you commit them to doing these things."

"Oh, darling, they will be fine with it, I'm sure." Lark continued to write as she spoke.

Dove stood. "I'm going to Brenda's house."

"You're leaving?"

"Yes. I think Brenda should be told in person." Dove walked into the living room as she heard her mother's chair move. Then her father's calming voice spoke.

"Let her go, Lark. She needs a little space."

"But family should be together at a time like this."

Dove looked over her shoulder at her father with thankful eyes, then walked out of the door.

The moment she sat inside her car the tears fell harder. All her life she had to deal with things as a loaner. Her mother was always loving, but a bit overbearing at times. Her father did a wonderful job as being the buffer when she was younger. As the teen years rolled in, it wasn't as easy to please his little girl. She was difficult and she knew it. It seemed the love between her parents was so strong she felt like a third wheel in her own home.

When her grandmother came to live with them she became Dove's solace. They would talk about any and everything, including her mother, but most of all their love for music. For the years she was with them, Sparrow was the mediator, the person who kept them together. Now that she was gone, Dove felt she was back to being the third wheel. Even now, her father's comfort went to his wife, her mother, as it should be. But who did she turn to? Who would be there to comfort her now that Grandma Sparrow was gone?

The thought tore at her heart. The pounding was so profound it felt as if it was tearing her chest apart. Just when she thought it was about to explode, Dove heard a tap at the top of her car. She looked out the windshield with tear filled eyes to see a stick hit the windshield. She wiped her face when she heard the tap again, then took a closer look. A black sparrow peeked at her from the roof of her car.

Dove stared back at the creature. It was as if the bird was looking directly into her eyes. Then it had the nerve to smile. How in the heck did a bird smile? The question crossed her mind as she tried to clear the unshed tears. She watched mesmerized as the bird walked down her windshield, turned then looked squarely in her eyes. The bird pecked once, then twice on the window.

Dove's heart eased. Her internal fears seemed to settle. A peace filled the car as she and the sparrow held each other's gaze.

"Hi, Grandma," Dove said.

The sparrow spread her wings, flew up a little as if suspended in front of the windshield. She pecked the window once more then flew away. Dove sat up leaning against the steering wheel as she stretched to watch the sparrow fly into a beautiful white cloud in the blue sky.

The bird had disappeared from her sight, but Dove remained sitting there. It dawned on her, if her heart was breaking, how much pain was her mother experiencing? She closed her eyes, took a deep breath, then stepped out of the car. Walking back into the house, she found her father placing a cup of tea on the table in front of her mother.

He looked up to see her standing there, smiled, then walked from the room.

Dove dropped her purse and walked into the kitchen singing one of the songs her mother would sing with her during better times, *Home* by Stephanie Mills.

Her mother turned towards her, surprise clearly etched on her face. Dove continued to sing as she took her mother's hand and pulled her to her feet. They began to sway as they did when she was little.

Lark's voice started weak as she joined Dove in song. It wasn't long before the silk voices began to blend. Lark's sultry voice mixed with Dove's soulful notes filled the air. Soon the feeling of love consumed the house in a way that only the universal sound of music can do. The two were dancing around the kitchen as if they were sisters rather than mother and daughter. Sharing each other's hurt, made it easier for them to deal with the loss of such an intricate part of their lives.

When they finished the song, they laughed and hugged. The hug led to heart wrenching tears.

"This is what Mother always wanted," Lark sniffed. "Us supporting each other in time of need."

"We need to follow her lessons," Dove added. "We need to be a family the way she taught us."

"From this moment on, we are going to honor her the same way she loved us."

Dove smiled. "Let's give her a worthy home-going. May I help you plan?"

"I would love that," Lark replied.

The two women sat down together and began the process of sending Sparrow home.

♩♩♩

At eighteen, Dove was a beautiful, warm golden brown-skinned young woman with the slim curvy body that would look good in a potato sack. She chose to keep her hair natural, using a flat iron when she wanted to wear it straight. Most times, she would unwind the pin-curls from the night before and let them fall where they may. Her grandmother liked her hair straight, so for today, she walked up to the microphone, pushed her shoulder length hair away from her face and begin to sing, acapella.

Dove began with *His Eye is on the Sparrow*, followed with *Take my Hand, Precious Lord*, and then she eased into *Summertime*. The audience was so caught up in her voice, few noticed the musicians moving to their instruments, which were on the podium behind her.

Her father and Rev. Paul left the stage to sit next to their wives in the audience. Everyone in the church stood, applauding at the completion of the song.

Dove acknowledged the applause as she and the choir began removing their robes.

The drummer began to play as she spoke.

"Anyone who truly knew my grandmother knew of her love for all music. The service is going to change to the songs my grandmother told me to sing when we sent her home."

The church was suddenly quiet. She belted out the strands of Percy Sledge's rendition of *When a Man Loves A Woman*. The musicians and choir joined in as she followed with Aaron Neville's *Tell It Like It Is, I Never Loved a Man The Way I Love You*, by Aretha Franklin. Then the audience came to their feet when the music for *Respect* by Re-Re broke out. Dancing in the aisles was encouraged as Dove pulled people to their feet. The church did not have time to settle down before Dove and the choir broke out in *Higher and Higher* by Jackie Wilson.

The pallbearers bobbed to the coffin, as the funeral director handed the floral bouquets to the flower girls. They danced down the aisle to the hearse waiting to carry Sparrow to her final resting place.

Things settled down at the burial site as Dove and Lark sang *Dream in Color* by Regina Belle. It was one of Sparrow's favorites from them. It was the song she felt conveyed the kind of love she had with her husband. She wanted her daughter and her granddaughter to have the same in their lives.

Sparrow St. Clair's homegoing service was packed. Friends and family from Georgia, North Carolina, and Virginia were there to celebrate the life of a woman who had touched them with her love of music. No one expected to receive a full-fledged musical tribute. Nor did Dove expect it to be a life-changing event. But that's what happened.

"That girl should be on somebody's stage getting paid for a performance like that, Martin," Rev. Paul said as they spoke at the grounds.

"That was Lark's dream. Dove never talked much about the limelight of the music world."

"Mother did," Lark commented. "Her dream was to sing at a presidential inauguration. When it didn't happen for her, she set her sights on me getting into the life."

"Why didn't you go all the way, Lark? You certainly have the voice."

Martin put his arms around her waist and pulled her close. "I take the blame."

"No, it wasn't on you, Martin. I made the choice to keep my life simple. I decided I wanted a love, not a host of lovers in my life. That is why I stayed home with you." She smiled at her husband who gently kissed her cheek. "Now Dove." Lark shook her head with a beaming smile. "She really has the pipes. We should encourage her to do something with that gift in the church more."

"I think it should be her choice," Martin stated. "Remember how you felt when your mother tried to push you into her dream. Don't make that mistake with Dove."

"Well, when God gives his gifts, He expects them to be used," Rev Paul stated. "Everyone who needs to be touched isn't always inside the church walls."

CHAPTER THREE

The repast was held at the church's family life center, which could easily hold up to five hundred people. Lark wasn't sure it was needed, until the family arrived following the burial. The place was packed. The atmosphere was festive, not solemn. That was a tribute to the way the services ended. Lark turned to her daughter and hugged her.

"Last part to this day," Lark said under her breath.

Dove squeezed her hand. "I meant Grandmother was going to leave us dancing to *Higher and Higher*."

"Your love keep lifting me higher, than I've ever been lifted before," Martin sang out.

"Sing it, baby." Lark smiled.

Martin shook his head blushing, waiving the request off. "I'll sing it to you later. Right now, I need you two to grab something to eat."

"We have you covered, Uncle Martin," Brenda guided them to a table. "Mother is instructing the kitchen crew to bring plates out for all of you."

"Huh, is the kitchen staff ready to quit?" Lark asked.

Brenda laughed. "Just about. I asked them to stay until you all arrived and was fed. With my mother around you never know what's going to happen."

"Thanks, Brenda," Dove hugged her. "Where are you sitting?"

Brenda did a little two-step. "I'm working the room, baby, I'm working the room."

Dove laughed, which she was certain Brenda was going for. Brenda St. Clair was her distant cousin. Her mom Carole and Dove's mom Lark were half-sisters. Her grandmother, Lark's mom, married Carole's father. They raised both girls. Brenda was Dove's cousin and closest friend.

She was blessed with the brains but she did not have a lyrical bone in her body. Brenda had just completed law school and was working in the District Attorney's office as an assistant DA.

It was at Brenda's house she stayed whenever she needed to get away. The night before her grandmother passed away she and her parents had a whopper of a disagreement. Dove declared on her eighteenth birthday that she would no longer sing in the choir. Lark wanted Dove to commit to doing a full tour with the church choir. She was done with the internal politics, the woman clambering for her father's attention just to get a solo in the program, and frustrated with the looks of anger each time she was asked to take the lead on a song. Her mother didn't care about any of that. Her opinion was simple, "You have a magnificent voice and it should be heard." She would always say, "It's their problem to deal with not yours." But it was her problem. She had to face the evil eyes of those members on Tuesday and Thursday nights during choir rehearsal. The looks knowing the song was selected for her voice because a VIP was attending church on a particular Sunday. Dove was aware of her talent; however, she knew others had talent, too. At times, she would try to step back and allow others to shine, but her mother would put her foot down with her father and Dove would always end up doing the solo. This time Dove put her foot down.

The showcase her father wanted to enter the choir in would have to win the $20,000 prize without her. And they could. That was what made the situation so frustrating. The choir was good with or without her. "But they are unbeatable with you," her mother had said. "Your father worked hard to build up the reputation of our choir. The St.Clair Belles have been at the top of the list for requests for years. You are going to do this for your father or you can leave this house." Dove chose to leave the house.

Brenda whispered in her ear, "Everything okay with you and Aunt Lark?"

Dove shrugged. "Haven't had much time to deal with everything."

"You rocked that church today. Don't you miss it?"

"I do." Dove smiled. "If my mother would just accept what I was willing to do, I'd be back singing next Sunday."

"Talk with her about it again. Try to get her to listen. But in the meantime, if you need a break you have the key."

"Thanks." Dove smiled as Brenda turned to walk away. "Oh, oh, oh, oh—you will never believe who was at Mama Sparrow's service."

"Who?"

"KJ Murphy."

"The producer?" Dove questioned with a bit of awe.

"None other," Brenda replied.

Lark turned to her daughter's raised voice. "From KJ Music? He was one of Mother's music students."

Dove and Brenda stared at Lark with mouths open.

"When?" Brenda asked, shocked at the information.

"Grandmother never said anything about KJ."

Lark shook her head. "She never called him that and neither did I."

"You know KJ?" Dove looked at her mother as if she was a totally different person. "You never mentioned him."

"Yes, I did."

"Mother." Dove put her purse on the table. "I have never heard you talk about KJ Murphy."

"I didn't call him that."

"What did you call him?" Brenda asked.

"Baby," Martin said in a disgusted tone Dove had never heard from her father before.

Brenda and Dove shared a glance as Lark kissed her husband's cheek.

"You're the only man for me," she said then wiped the lipstick from his face.

"Mother," Dove laughed. "You and KJ?"

"No," Lark proclaimed.

"Not the place or time," Martin suggested with a stern look at his daughter.

"Funerals and weddings." Brenda shook her head with laughter.

"What?" Dove turned to her cousin.

"That's when all the little secrets surface, wedding and funerals."

Dove laughed as a plate of food was placed in front of her. "Girl you made me feel like dancing up in that church today." Her Aunt Carole did a little dance step. "Mama Sparrow is smiling down at us." She held her hand up to the sky.

"Yes, she is," Lark said as she began to eat.

Twenty minutes later a buzz began around the room. Dove was talking with a few people at another table when Kenneth Jordan Murphy entered the room dressed in a skinny suit looking like a million-dollars.

She watched as he made a beeline towards her mother, but was blocked by Aunt Carole.

"Can I help you, Kenneth?" The tone was not pleasant.

"No," he stated then walked around her.

Aunt Carole gave him a side eye as he continued towards her mother's table. When her hands went to her hips and the arm started flinging with the walk, Dove knew something was up. Aunt Carole approached and was blocked by two rather healthy built men as KJ proceeded on.

Her mother continued to talk with the woman in front of her as Dove watched her father move to greet KJ. The look on her father's face was pleasant, but not at all welcoming. That was unusual for him. Dove excused herself then walked towards the small group, who had captured the attention of the just about everyone in the reception hall.

"Kenneth." Martin extended his hand. "Thank you for coming."

KJ nodded as he shook her father's hand. "Paying my respects."

"We appreciate it," Martin replied.

"Yes, well, you've paid your respects, now you can go," Aunt Carole politely suggested as she finally made her way around the men.

Dove didn't miss the tension in the room. She looked around to capture Brenda's eye. When she did Dove nodded towards the small group. They both met at her father's side. Martin took her hand.

"This is our daughter, Dove. Dove, Mr. Murphy."

"Hello Mr. Murphy. It's nice to meet you."

He took her hand. "The pleasure is mine. In fact, you are the reason I delayed my departure." He brought her hand up.

Martin pulled it away before it reached his lips. "Why is that?" he asked as he pushed Dove a step behind him.

Sensing a problem rising, Dove reached behind him to touch her mother's arm.

Lark looked around, excused herself from the woman she was talking to then stood next to her husband.

"Songbird." KJ grinned.

"Her name is Lark Warren," Martin corrected.

Lark smiled. "Hello, Kenneth." He held his arms out to her. She laughed. "Not happening. Do you remember the last time you tried that in front of my husband Martin? You do remember Martin, don't you?"

KJ chuckled. "I do. No disrespect, Martin." He turned back to Lark. "I am sorry to hear about Mrs. Sparrow. She was special."

"She was." Lark nodded her head. "It was nice of you to come."

Dove glance at Brenda. They both grinned at the scene unfolding in front of them.

"Mrs. St. Clair was the one person who never let me get away with crap. She taught me how to appreciate my talent and how to handle the business of music. I owe her."

"Grandmother, really?"

His eyes went to Dove. "She did and in return I would like to do that for you." KJ reached back to one of the men who entered the room with him. The man placed a card in his hand. "You have a beautiful voice and stage presence." He gave the card to Dove. "You have...it. Call me. I would love an opportunity to talk about your future."

Dove took the card and smiled. “Thank you.” Then she gave the card to her father. “I am honored, Mr. Murphy.”

“KJ, please.”

“Thank you, Mr. Murphy,” Dove replied sensing the heat coming from her father.

“Your mother turned her back on a music career. Have you considered what you want to do with your voice in the future?”

“Well, my parents have always handled decisions regarding my music. I’m afraid you will have to deal with them on the topic of my future.”

Brenda pinched her and frowned. Dove knew why. KJ Murphy was the owner and one of the best producers of the KJ Music Empire. Every artist he touches ends up with platinum on his or her walls. However, there was something between KJ and her parents she would need to understand before talking with him about music or anything else. They knew him, she didn’t.

KJ’s eyes turned from hers, to her father’s. “Martin, you know my work. You know her voice. I can take her to the top. Think about it and call me.” He shook her father’s hand then pointed to her mother. “May I?”

Martin nodded.

KJ smiled, then hugged her mother. “It was good seeing you.” He stepped back. “I hope to hear from both of you soon. And you.” He smiled at Dove. “This time next year I will have you in the spotlight. Embrace your gift. Mrs. Sparrow would want you to.” KJ turned and walked away.

Dove watched as people surrounded him, clamoring for autographs and taking pictures.

"Aunt Lark, you been keeping secrets, and Uncle Martin," Brenda raised an eyebrow, "it seems we have to talk."

"About?" Martin raised an eyebrow.

"About whatever you did to KJ when he hugged Mother." Dove grinned at her parents. She watched as they clasped their hands together and looked at each other.

"Grown folks' business," Lark said as the two of them turned and walked away.

"That story would burn up the pages of a book, if it was ever told," Aunt Carole said, then walked off with her hips and arms swaying in rhythm.

CHAPTER FOUR

KJ lived up to his word. Six months after her grandmother's death, Dove was doing guest spots on major artists' songs, performing on stage with them and doing live interviews. She was so good that a number of artists refused to have her on their CDs. While Dove was devastated, KJ found it humorous.

"Songbird II, it's time. You need to make the move to Atlanta and go solo. I'll smooth things over with your parents."

"You are going to convince my dad to let me move to Atlanta with you?" Dove laughed. "I want to see that happen."

"When I do, don't come here getting mixed up with some guy that's going to bring you down."

"Why would you think I would do that?"

KJ rolled his eyes heavenward. "I've sung that song and did that dance many times before. I know how that record ends."

"Well, I don't foresee that happening, Mr. Murphy, but if it does, I'm sure you will find a way to pull me away before any damage is done."

KJ flew into Richmond the next day, met with Martin and Lark for hours before they agreed. The next month Dove moved to an apartment in the Buckhead area of Atlanta. She had a car, but liked taking the Marta System to the studio. Met her project team manager and was on her way to stardom.

Working under the stage name of Bell St. Clair, Dove released her first solo project titled, Driven. It remained in the number one spot on the Billboard 200 for 62 weeks, with four singles, including the title track, hitting the Hot 100 for 20 weeks or more at a time. Within two years Dove had become simply Belle. Her photos were on billboards, magazines, and every social media platform known to mankind. Her star power rating was still climbing, according to KJ. It was during that time Dove learned there were two sides to the music world: the side of the limelight and fans, and the side with deals, contracts and disappointment.

Trevor Allen Thomas, better known to the public as TAT the rapper, requested a collaboration with Dove.

TAT was considered to be one of the top rappers in the world. His rhymes appeared in commercials, was used for the introductions for NBA All Star games, NFL playoff teams, you name it, his raps were legendary.

They met in the studio while collaborating on a song called Lyrics where he did the rap and Dove did the chorus. The song broke records on just about every musical chart, even country. The two toured together, held appearances together and eventually became the talk of the music industry.

To the public TAT and Belle were on top of the world. But where Dove had a clear idea of what she wanted in her career, TAT's vision was for her to do his songs. The more she told him that wasn't what she wanted, the more controlling TAT became.

"I want to sing the national anthem at a Presidential Inauguration. I think it would be a great way to honor my grandmother," she said one day.

TAT laughed. In fact, he laughed so hard his boys, who seemed to always be around, joined in.

"Who in the hell do you think you are, Whitney or Bey?" He smirked. "You got a voice. But you ain't got it like that."

The words cut deep. "At least I have a dream," she replied and walked out.

The next day, she shared the conversation with KJ.

"I distinctly remember telling you not to get involved with anyone who would bring you down. If he don't believe in your dream, he doesn't believe in you."

"Do you?" Dove asked. "Do you believe in my dream?"

"I've heard this dream from your grandmother and then your mother." He glanced up at her for a second then back to the console. "Is this your dream or theirs?"

Tilting her head to the side she thought. "This one is all me. I believe I could get an invitation to sing at the next inauguration. What do you think?"

"I know you can." He nodded without even looking up from the console. "Let's change up your next project. Make it a soulful sound like some Regina Belle, a little Mariah, and yes, let's add some Whitney in there. I'll have the marketing people hook you up with a few of the NFL teams to sing the national anthem at a few of the games."

"You can make that happen?"

"Yeah, I can make it happen. You may have to back up on the rap stuff with TAT a little. Will that cause problems for you two?"

"There really isn't an us." Dove shrugged. "We have different plans for my life."

"Do you love him? I not talking the puppy love thing, I'm talking your parents' kind of love?"

"No." Dove sighed, not expounding on the reply. She pushed a button. "I want to warm up with this today." She walked into the booth, put on the headphones, and listened as the music filled the room. Dove began to sing Regina Belle's song *Dream in Color*. The words *I want a love, not just a lover,* resonated in her soul and she knew what she had to do.

Breaking things off with TAT came sooner than she expected. During a release party for one of KJ's other artists, TAT and Dove sat in a booth talking with a few friends. TAT mentioned his next CD and a few songs he had in mind for them to do together. Dove waited until his friends got up to dance to hold TAT back.

"TAT, I'm going into the studio to begin my next solo project with KJ. I won't be available for your next project."

"That ain't happening. In fact, I think it's time you let KJ go and sign with me."

"What?" Dove laughed. "TAT, you want me to give up my solo career to be second on your tracks? Why would I do that?"

"Because I said you would."

"To who?"

"People I'm building my label with."

"You need to tell them you were mistaken. I'm staying with KJ Music."

"Not happening. Like I said, you're with me." He put his arms around her.

Dove slipped from under his arms. "This is where I get off, TAT. It's time for me to work on my dreams."

TAT made the mistake of grabbing Dove a little too forcefully. “Don’t start with me.”

Dove pulled away. “No, TAT. I’m done. You’re going to have to find someone else to play your girl role.” She turned to walk away.

TAT followed, grabbing her. “Get your ass back here.”

One of the security team members alerted KJ to the situation.

“Is everything okay?” KJ asked as he approached them and smoothly moved Dove aside.

“Step off, man. This is between me and my woman,” TAT barked in KJ’s face.

“TAT, she’s my responsibility. *You* know that.” KJ took Dove’s hand.

TAT pulled her back toward him.

“I’m okay, Mr. Murphy.” Dove tried to intervene.

“TAT, we don’t do this in public. Let me take Dove home and you two can talk tomorrow.”

“Did you put this solo crap in her head?” TAT demanded. At the rise of his voice, his boys gathered at his side.

“I don’t talk business in public.“ KJ reached out. “Let’s go, Dove.”

“Get your hands off her,“ TAT pushed KJ in the chest. “Your business with her is over. She’s signing an exclusive contract with me.”

KJ’s security moved between him and TAT.

“No, I’m not, TAT,” Dove told him again.

He jerked around, yelling in her face. “Shut the hell up.”

“Look, I don’t know if you’re drunk, high or sipping your own Kool-aid, but my father’s name is Martin,” Dove responded while backing away from him.

TAT grabbed her by the hair.

"Take him down," KJ ordered.

While his security team stepped into action. KJ picked Dove up and carried her from the club as cell phone cameras flashed away.

♩♩♩

Dove woke up the next morning to her phone buzzing. She reached over and put it to her ear. "Hello," she answered in a groggy voice.

"Warning, warning, warning. Your parents are on their way to Atlanta."

"What?" Dove sat straight up in bed, brushing her hair back from her face.

"TAT got arrested and is there something romantic going on with you and KJ? What the hell?" Brenda yelled into the phone.

"No there is nothing going on with me and Mr. Murphy. We got into an argument and he intervened."

"You and *who* got into an argument?"

"TAT... me and TAT got into an argument."

"Well, your parents flew out at 7:15 this morning. They will be knocking on your door shortly."

"Wait, how do you know about this?"

"It's all over social media, pictures and all."

Dove grabbed her tablet off the nightstand, turned it on then googled her name. "Oh no."

"You have it?" Brenda asked through the phone, which Dove now had on speaker. "If not, I can send you plenty of links."

"TAT got arrested? People got hurt?"

"You sound like you weren't there."

"KJ got me out just when things went crazy."

"Well, it's a good thing he did," Brenda said. "According to the news report, TAT had a gun. That's why he got arrested."

"He always carrying, Brenda. That's nothing new."

She was silent for a moment. “Dove, don’t tell anyone else that.”

“I’m sure he has a permit.”

“I’m just as sure he doesn’t,” Brenda countered. “TAT is a felon. If he gets anywhere near a gun, he is looking at five years federal time.”

“What?”

“Just don’t tell anyone else what you just told me.”

Her phone buzzed. Dove looked at the phone. “Oh no, they’re here.”

“Have fun.” Brenda laughed then hung up.

“Hi, Mother.” She tried to sound cheery and normal.

“We are at the airport. I don’t know what’s going on, Dove Sinclair Warren, but your father is very upset and so am I. We’ll be at your place in twenty minutes. Be ready to answer some questions, young lady.”

“Yes, ma’am.” Dove hung up, then dialed KJ’s number. “Good morning. I am so sorry.”

“You have nothing to be sorry for. Last night was on TAT, not you,” KJ replied.

“I’m not talking about last night.”

“What are you talking about?”

“My parents are here. They are on their way to my place.” There was a moment of hesitation. “Mr. Murphy?”

KJ laughed. “It’s Mr. Murphy when you’re in trouble. I’ll be there in an hour. Try to keep your father calm until I get there.”

After Martin and Lark watched the surveillance tape from the club, for the third time, they were convinced about KJ’s take on what happened. Dove sat quietly as KJ explained how his PR team was handling the situation.

"I don't want her reputation ruined over a bar brawl," Martin declared.

"It wasn't a bar, Dad," Dove explained. "It was a club and we were there for a release party. No, I was not drinking and no, I don't do drugs for the umpteenth time."

"What was the argument about?" Lark asked.

"I told TAT that I wasn't singing on his next project. He said he wants me to leave Mr. Murphy and sign exclusively with his label."

"Did you tell him you would do that?" Martin asked.

"No. I told him I would not do that and that I was staying with Mr. Murphy. That's when he got all mad and grabbed me."

"I stepped in at that point," KJ added as he sat up. "Dove, you should go pack a bag. I think you should go home with your parents until I clear things up."

Dove sighed. "I think I should call TAT and smooth things over with him."

"I don't think that's a good idea," KJ countered. "In fact, I don't think TAT needs to know where you are for a while."

"So, I'm supposed to just disappear now. What about my next project?"

"That is still going to happen. Nothing has changed with that. In fact, while you're home, you will be working on music for that project. Don't think you are on a vacation."

"But..."

"Your career is about longevity. Go home. I'll work on things for the next project."

Dove looked from KJ to her parents.

"Go pack," her father said.

"I'll help you." Lark stood, patted her husband's hand then walked with Dove to the other room.

KJ waited, then motioned for Martin to join him in the kitchen. "TAT is mixed up with some shady people. I don't want Dove around him."

"Why would you put my daughter with someone like him? She's a songstress and had no business playing second to some rapper."

"Let's be very clear, Martin. The collaboration with TAT was great for Dove, hell, for them both. It put her on a higher plain and improved his reputation. I had nothing to do with them getting together in any other way. That happened on its own."

"You should have broken it up before it got this far."

"It's been my experience not to tell a teenager not to do anything. They will only go in the direction you don't want them to go." He shrugged. "As it turned out, Dove is a smart girl. She discovered on her own that TAT was not good for her."

"And you?"

KJ shook his head. "Martin, you know I would never look at Dove in that way or you wouldn't have sent her here."

Martin sighed. "So, what do we do?"

"Exactly what Dove and I talked about, get her ready for her next solo project." He hesitated. "You have somewhere in Richmond she can stay where TAT can't easily find her?"

Martin thought for a moment. "You think he may come for her?"

"I do."

"Then she should come home where we can protect her."

"Your house will be the first place TAT will look. She talks about her cousin Brenda. Can she stay there?"

"Of course, she can. Does TAT know about Brenda?"

"I don't think they had that kind of a relationship," KJ replied.

"The internet made it seem like they were practically living together."

"No, in fact I made it a point that Dove was to come home every night."

Martin smiled. "Thank you for that."

KJ nodded. "She's Lark's daughter. It's the same as if she was mine."

Martin straightened at the statement. "But, she's not. Dove and Lark belong to me."

KJ nodded. "You're a lucky bastard. Let's get her back to Richmond as soon as possible."

CHAPTER FIVE

Anthony Perry was sitting in his office overlooking the city preparing documents for court. Tony, as his friends called him, was the DA for the city of Richmond. Tony was serious about everything. Losing two brothers to the streets, one in a drive by shooting and the other to drugs, made him hard-hearted and more determined to do well in his chosen profession.

Tony's mom, Elaine, wanted at least one of her children to do something positive with their life. Two sons buried and a daughter still trying to find herself was more than one mother should have to bear. Determined to have one child do well, Elaine worked two jobs to keep Tony in college and then law school. The family sacrifice paid off when Tony passed the bar and landed a job in the Henrico County District Attorney's office. Now, two years later at the age of twenty-nine, he was the District Attorney of Richmond. God had indeed been good to him. Tony never forgot the sacrifice they made for him. A step on his door made him look up.

"Hey, Tony, what are you doing this weekend?" Brenda St. Clair, one of his co-workers asked.

"No plans," Tony replied as he turned. "You have something in mind?"

"Funny, you should ask. My cousin is home from Atlanta and hanging out with me for a while. I was inviting a few friends over to meet her. Would you like to join us?"

"Sure, why not. What time?"

"Any time after work. We may pull out a deck of cards or two." She smiled.

Tony sat back at his desk and laughed. "You are certain you want me to come? If I remember correctly, I kind of wiped the table with your boy, Tim."

"I'm certain he would object to your analogy."

"The objection would be overturned, due to the pesky thing called facts."

"Why do you have to always pull the facts card. Just show up ready to play."

"I'm ready-always ready. I'll see you then."

Brenda rolled her eyes, then closed the door as she left.

Tony went back to the file on his desk, smiling. He wasn't much for hanging out with co-workers, but Brenda was good people. She was one of the only ADAs that willingly helped him orientate himself to the job when he first arrived. Knowing several of the ADAs in the office were in line for the position, he dealt with the bad feelings and the hesitation of being accepted into the brotherhood of the office. However, Tony did not let that concern him. As long as each ADA did their job, he was good. He was there to do a job, not make friends.

Tony's cell phone chimed. He checked his watch, it was after five. He answered.

"Tony, are you coming by the house before you go home today?"

"Hey, Mom, I had plans this evening. Did you need something?"

"Yeah, your sister wanted to know if you were going to drop a check off for her electric bill."

Tony closed his eyes, frustrated, but made certain his mother did not hear it in his voice. "Sure, Mom, I'll drop it off as soon as I leave here."

"Thank you, son. I truly appreciate it."

"I know, Mom. I'll see you soon."

Tony disconnected the call, packed up his desk, turned off the lights in the office and headed towards the bank of elevators. He worked on the third floor of City Hall, where there was a wealth of female employees. Once a group of men who worked in the building determined the ratio of women to men was five-to-one. Two from the more populated side of the ratio was walking towards him now. The look, and brief whisper between them indicated he was on their radar.

Today he wore a navy-blue suit with a gold and navy tie, and a lightly starched white shirt. The suit looked good on his six-two, one hundred ninety-five-pound body, with his low haircut and clean-shaven face. He knew it and so did they.

When the elevator arrived, he held the door open to allow the two women inside. One smiled.

"Thank you, Mr. Perry," the first one said as she entered the elevator. The other nodded, then followed her inside.

"You're welcome and the name is Tony," he replied as he pushed the button for the lobby.

He stepped to the side as the other woman tilted her head.

"We are having drinks at Havana. Would you like to join us?"

The elevator stopped and the doors opened.

"I have plans for the night. Rain check?"

The ladies stepped out as he held the doors open for them.

"Another time," the woman replied over her shoulder as she smiled back at him.

Tony acknowledged her with a slight nod of his head. "Another time." He stopped at the ATM machine near the main entrance of the building as the ladies continued out the door. It was nice to draw ladies' attention every now and then. It let him know he was still in the game. A game he was losing, but still a player.

When he reached his mom's house, his sister Karen was already there.

Tony chuckled. "Just as I thought. She needed weekend party money."

Tony parked behind the used SUV he purchased for Karen a year ago, in the driveway of the house he purchased for his mom when he was hired as DA. He enjoyed having the ability to help his family. He understood life could have turned out very different for him if it had not been for their sacrifice. Tony did not take his position in life for granted. He knew how to give back to the community and it started with his family.

"Hey, where is everyone?" Tony called out as he entered the unlocked front door.

"Anthony, we are in the kitchen," Elaine's voice rang out.

Tony walked into the kitchen to find his mother at the stove cooking and Karen at the kitchen table peeling potatoes. "Hey, Mom," he said as he hugged her and sniffed. "Cornbread smells good." He walked over to the table and tapped Karen on the head. "Hey, Peewee."

"Boy, don't you mess up my hair," Karen joked.

"Here." Tony gave the envelope with the money from the ATM to Karen. "I put a little extra in there for you. Have some fun."

"Thanks, Tony, I'll pay you back." Karen smiled.

"Yeah, yeah, the week after never," he teased. "Where are the kids?"

"Jasmine is upstairs on the phone, of course. The boys are out back. They love that backyard," Karen huffed.

"I'll be back," Tony said as he ran out the back door to play with her boys, Tye, age three and Javon, age five.

"Mom, will you look at them." Karen smiled as she watched her brother from the French doors leading to the patio. "Tony is nothing but a big kid."

"That boy needs a wife and a house full of children." Elaine laughed.

"I agree, but it has to be someone special. Not just anybody. Whoever gets my brother better be worthy or it ain't happening."

Tony came in the house with Tye in his arms and Javon holding on to his leg.

"Alright, go wash up for dinner."

The boys ran through the house towards the bathroom as instructed.

"You know you should not be out there rolling around in the dirt in your work clothes. That white shirt is going to get grass stains on it." Elaine scowled. "Are you staying for dinner?"

"No, I have plans tonight," Tony replied.

"Who's the lucky lady?" Karen asked with a smirk. "You've been playing solo for a while since Stephanie got married."

Tony frowned at Karen. "That was cute." Tony knew with the mention of Stephanie, his mom was about to go in on him.

"I don't know why you didn't marry that girl. She would have been a good wife to you," Elaine huffed with a shake of her head.

Tony gave Karen the evil eye. "I wasn't feeling it, Mom," he said as he kissed her on the forehead. "I have to go. I'll talk to you later, evil," he said to Karen.

Karen stuck her tongue out at him as he left the room.

♩♩♩

"Fazi, it's Lou from Atlanta. How's it hanging?"

"Lou," Fazi leaned back in his big leather chair with a big grin on his face. "Long time no hear."

"Fire's hot here in Atlanta."

"Is that so? What can I do for here in cool Richmond?"

"I need location and surveillance on one Belle St. Clair."

Fazi sat up. "The singer? That's a hot number for sure. You think she's here in Richmond?"

"Her family's from there."

"Get out of dodge?"

"I can see you're not up on the latest pop news."

"No, Michael Bouble is as far pop as I go." He laughed. "Send me photos of St. Clair and whatever contact info you have. We'll locate her. Usual fee?"

"On this we'll double the fee. We may need more from you."

"Send the info and keep me posted."

"Will do."

Fazi pulled the picture sent by Lou up on his phone. "Whoa, she's a looker." He passed the phone to one of his men. "This is our target. Find her and keep her under wraps."

"You got it, boss."

CHAPTER SIX

Tony went home, which was about fifteen minutes away from his mom's house. He lived in the exclusive Highlight District apartment complex downtown. It was a set of restored warehouses turned luxury apartments, located close enough to the court house for him to walk. The city's nightlife was within minutes of where he lived, but inside the apartment complex you would never know it.

You literally stepped into another world when you entered the lobby of his building, with its marble floors, high-end finishes and an indoor-outdoor restaurant and bar. As for his apartment, from the hallway the door opened directly to the hardwood parquet floor, which seems to flow on forever and ended with a breath-taking view of the river and the skyline of the Southside of the city. The foyer flowed into the great room, which was furnished with black leather furniture and a glass table top. One sofa faced the view of the river and the other sofa faced the marble fireplace. The dining room was to the right of the room with a glass topped and brass table with black and white cloth covered chairs. A hallway separated the top-of-the-line appliance filled kitchen and the huge great room.

Tony placed his keys in the tray on the breakfast bar at the entrance of the kitchen, then headed to the staircase that led to a huge open-lofted bedroom on the second level. The room to the left of the staircase was a walk-in closet. Tony stripped out of his clothes, bagged them in the labeled container and placed them in the laundry drop. He walked into the bathroom and turned on the water to the walk-thru shower stall, next to the whirlpool tub and an enclosed lavatory.

Stepping out, he lotioned his body down with one percent baby oil, washed his face, then brushed his teeth. Convinced the oil was now dry on his skin, he dressed in a pair of tan linen-silk blend trousers with a cashmere pullover sweater that revealed a well-defined body, tan loafers and his leather jacket.

Tony walked out of the closet, took a quick peek in the full-length mirror in the corner of his bedroom and declared himself ready for the night. The thing about Brenda's house is you never knew who you might meet. She knew a lot of people and they had no problem showing up in numbers, even for a simple get together. To be honest, he knew Brenda's friend Timothy would be there. Tim was always hooked up and ready to rag on whatever Tony decided to wear. Yes, men dress for other men, just like women dress to impress other women.

There were a number of vehicles at Brenda's house when Tony arrived. He grabbed the bottle of wine out the back seat, walked up to the front porch and rang the doorbell.

"Man, I'm glad to see you, these women are trying to wear me out," Tim greeted when he opened the door. "Come on in."

"What's up, Tim?" Tony said as he shook his hand. "They're giving you a hard time, man?"

"Trying to, bro, and Brenda's the worst one"

"Cry baby," Brenda said as she walked up the steps to the foyer. "Pay him no mind, Tony, come on in. Let me introduce you to one or two people."

Brenda grabbed Tony by the arm, retreating to the lower level family room that housed the bar, pool table on one side and the theater room with the big screen and leather seating for six in the other room.

"Everybody, Tony... Tony, everybody"

The people in the room yelled, "Tony."

Tony yelled back to the approximately ten people in the room, "Everybody."

At the bar were two women, one of which was the woman Tony had taken the elevator trip with earlier in the day.

"Well, hello again." she was in full flirt mood as he approached.

Tony smiled and extended his hand. "Rain check came in sooner than I expected. You know my name and you are?"

"Linda Campbell."

"So, you two have met?" Brenda asked.

"Not exactly," Tony replied. "We had an elevator trip together."

"An enjoyable one, I might add." Linda patted the seat.

"Linda is the new ADA in the gang division," Brenda stated.

"Rough area," Tony commented, knowing the fact that she worked in the DA's office put her off limits. Tony did not date women he worked with, not even for one night stands. It was one of his golden rules.

"I'm a tough lady," she replied.

He knew that was a lead in, but he had to let it pass. "You are going to have to be tough to work with that group." He used that moment to bow out. "Listen, I'm going to talk to Tim for a minute, would you ladies excuse me?" Tony did not give either lady a chance to answer, he simply walked away.

"Tony, you remember Joe from the last time we played Bid Whist and ran a Boston on him?" Tim laughed, then became serious. "Yeah, he wants another ass whipping."

"You know, Joe, I honestly thought it was clear we were the superior team the last time we played," Tony laughed.

"I had the wrong partner the last time," Joe countered. "Get me a decent partner I'll show you something."

"Hey, do we have any bid whist players in the house?" Tony asked.

"I can hang with Spades," Linda replied.

"No, baby, we are talking about a grown man's game," Tim replied with a chuckle.

"Dove is upstairs," Brenda threatened. "You know she has whipped your ass many times at your man's game."

"That was luck," Tim replied, then turned away. "Okay, Joe, you can have Tony as your partner, I'll take Dove." He then ran off shouting, "Let's take this to the kitchen where we can play undisturbed."

Brenda's house was a tri-level; the family room where most of the guests were, was located on the bottom level. Joe headed towards the bar for drinks as Tony and Tim walked up six steps that led to the foyer, then six more steps that led to the second level of the house. The living room, dining room, a small office, and the kitchen were on that level. Tim pointed Tony and Joe to the kitchen as he headed up the next eight steps that led to the third level and all four bedrooms.

"You set up the table," Joe stated as he turned back. "I'll get a few bottles from the bar for the game."

Tony took off his jacket, placed it on the arm of the sofa then proceeded through the dining room to reach the kitchen. As he entered he found someone standing in a chair trying to reach something in the cabinet above the refrigerator. At first sight, Tony thought it was a little girl. Then he noticed the pink toenails. His eyes traveled up her jean covered legs, over the shapely behind, to the waist uncovered by the midriff top that led to a bust line that could only belong to a full-grown woman. His body's reaction to the full picture indicated the vision before him was definitely not a little girl. Looking down to clear his mind of the thoughts raging through, Tony noticed the chair was about to come from under her as she leaned further forward.

"Do you need some help?" Tony asked.

She turned a little too fast. The movement tilted the chair, pushing it from under her.

Reaching for but missing the bottom of the cabinet for leverage, the box she had grabbed and her body, arms swinging for balance, was out of control. Tony ran forward catching her spiraling body just before she hit the floor.

She did not weight a lot, but the fall propelled them both backwards. Tony landed on the floor with her on his chest and the Fruity Pebbles box flying across the kitchen floor.

The woman let out a little scream and a huff as she realized she survived the fall.

"Well," she sat up as she pushed her hair from her face, "that just happened."

Tony laid there, staring at the face of an angel. Or was it her voice that made the heavens sing. He wasn't sure.

Brenda came running into the room along with some of the other guests.

"What on earth is going on?" Brenda asked as she extended a hand. "Dove, are you okay?"

"I think so." Dove checked her arms then looked at the man who broke her fall. "Are you okay?"

At first, he wondered if she realized she was sitting, literally sitting, on top of the part of his anatomy that was responding to her nearness. Then he wondered if she could feel his response to her. It was then that the blush turned her face crimson red. He had his answer.

She took Brenda's hand and stood looking down at him.

"I'm so sorry." She brushed her hair back as she reached her hand down to help him up.

"Other than a broken back and an embarrassed moment, I'm fine." Tony laughed as he took her hand. *She was pretty strong for a little thing,* he thought.

"I see you found Dove." Tim laughed as he walked into the kitchen. The other people went back to the individual areas once the excitement died down.

"What were you doing?" Brenda asked Dove.

"I was hungry," Dove replied as she walked over to pick up the box of cereal.

"Dove did you not see all this on the counter top?" Brenda asked.

"Yes, but I wanted the Fruity Pebbles you keep hiding from me," Dove replied, giving Brenda a look of defiance.

Brenda grabbed the box. "Give me that box. Your mother is not going to get on me if you gain weight."

Dove grabbed the box back from Brenda. "She's not here and what she doesn't know will not hurt her." She reached into the box and stuffed some of the dry cereal in her mouth.

Brenda laughed and Dove joined in.

"I am sorry." Dove looked up at Tony who was watching the scene with amusement. "Thank you for catching me. It was your voice that caught me off guard and caused the fall." She smiled. "Are you sure you're okay?"

For a long moment, Tony stared at her. Then he realized she had asked a question. "Yes, I'm fine."

"Good." Dove held his gaze for a long moment before turning away. She smiled. "I'm going back upstairs."

"No-no, I was up there looking for you. We need a fourth person for Bid Whist," Tim declared. "You can't go back to your room now."

"Tim, I'm sorry I can't. I'll have to pass this time. I have a conference call with Mr. Murphy in a few minutes." She put her hands on her hips and smirked. "Besides I distinctly remember you telling me I could never play cards in this house again after the last time I beat you."

"You were lucky, that's all, lucky," Tim taunted.

"You call it luck. I call it skills. I got skills baby," she laughed as Brenda and Tony joined in.

"Don't do it, Tony." Tim shook his head. "Where's your male pride?"

"I'm just here to play the game, man." Tony threw his hands up, folded his arms across his chest, leaned back against the counter top to take in his fill of the woman named Dove.

She was staring at him. Tony recognized the look for he was sending the same look of admiration her way.

"I'm sorry, you two haven't met." Brenda's voice disturbed his thoughts and the wave of her hand interrupted his vision. "Tony."

He finally looked up at her. "Yes?"

"This is my cousin, Dove. Dove, this is my boss Anthony Perry," she said as she pulled a bowl of fruit from the refrigerator and placed it on the table. Then she took the box of cereal from her once again. "Both is full of sugar. This is just better for you."

Dove huffed then reached for his hand. "It's nice to meet you, Mr. Perry. I apologize again for the circumstances."

He waited for the smile to appear, but she jerked her hand away as if he had burned her. "I have to go back to work now; excuse me."

Tony's eyes followed Dove's retreating body and saw when she glanced back over her shoulder to look at him as she left the room. His estimation of her was about 5'4, 110 lbs., most of which was her butt that was making her jeans scream, light brown skin complexion with a little more than shoulder length brown hair, and brown eyes.

He turned back to find Brenda watching him.

She shook her head and laughed. "Why do men always want the ones they have no chance in hell of getting?"

"What?"

"What my ass." Brenda chuckled. "Since you can't get your card game going, how about a game of pool, Tony?"

"Sounds like a plan to me." Tony smiled, glancing over his shoulder in the direction of the fallen angel, then followed Brenda into the other room.

CHAPTER SEVEN

The next morning Dove sat in the kitchen at the table waiting for Brenda to get up. It was a Saturday. The one day during the week she could sleep late. The last thing Dove wanted to do was wake her up for a workout. She used the time to check the internet for stories mentioning her or TAT. It was now two weeks since the fight and five days since the last mention of her name with TAT. Whatever KJ's team was doing seemed to be working. TAT's threatening calls had stopped three days ago. The last call indicated she would pay for everyday he spent in jail unless she agreed to sign with his label. She hadn't mentioned the threats to anyone hoping he would stop.

Dove checked the clock on the wall again. It was now seven in the morning. Her workout was usually completed by this time. She realized the mini retreat from the limelight was more than needed.

For the last three years, Dove had gone non-stop from working in the studio, to video tapings, to interviews, to promotional tours, to live performances. She was about to reach her twenty-first birthday and felt like she had worked a lifetime. KJ was right, the break had cleared her mind giving her the vision on how she could fulfill her grandmother's dream.

Blessed with good looks, the voice of an angel and a mother with the drive and determination to make her a star, Dove knew more was needed; the desire had to be in her heart. As her grandmother would say, love is the driving force to accomplish your dreams. Dove hadn't done much other than what came naturally. Singing was like breathing to her; however, there was a missing element. She didn't know what or how to determine what was missing. *You'll know when it appears*, her grandmother's voice played in her head. *You'll know*. She had to trust and believe, the missing element will show up when it was needed. For now, she was going to work with KJ on selecting the right music to get her to the next level and pray that TAT and his people would leave her alone.

The doorbell interrupted her thoughts. Dove listened for movement from the upstairs, there was nothing. She put her tablet on the table then glanced over the bannister to look out of the window. Through the double doors Dove could see it was the good-looking brother that broke her fall the night before.

She wondered if Brenda was expecting him or did he just show up. Her stomach flipped at the sight of him. She could sit back and just look at him for hours with his mocha smooth skin, those intelligent eyes, cleft chin and thick mouthwatering lips, not to mention his tall muscular body. She bet he was a runner. Her hands went to her hair, smoothing it in place. She grimaced thinking she didn't have on any makeup or decent clothes. She was dressed in sweats and a hat for the anticipated run with Brenda.

The bell sounded again. Walking down the stairs she began talking to herself. Every step towards the door made her skin tingle. "I can do this," she said. "He's just a man, A good-looking man, but still just a man." She stopped, took a deep breath, then opened the door. Looking at him her grandmother's words, *as good as a smooth chocolate Hersey bar*, came to mind.

"Good morning." She smiled.

He turned towards her with a surprised look on his face. Time suspended. Dove couldn't help staring at him. It seemed his face brightened the day even though the sun was already shining. Then he smiled and she had the urge to giggle. It was something about his smile that soothed her like being in her grandmother's lap in the rocker used to do.

"Good morning."

His gaze lingered over her causing moisture to form in regions she couldn't believe. *Is that possible from a smile*? She thought. Say something. No, I don't need to say anything. He came to the house... right. Her mind was all confused.

"Are you here to see Brenda?" she stammered.

"Excuse me?"

It eased her tension to realize she wasn't they only one confused. "Brenda... are you here to see Brenda?"

"Yes." He released nervous laughter.

Beautiful white teeth appeared between those thick lips. Involuntarily, her tongue slid between her lips. She caught the action before he noticed, she hoped.

"I think she is still asleep, may I help you with something?"

His tongue snaked out, moistening his lips. "I need to pick up my jacket I left here last night."

Dove had only met him last night, but she had no idea how close he was to Brenda. She wasn't sure if she should just let him in. "Do you remember where you put your jacket?" she asked.

"On the sofa in the living room next to the kitchen."

"Okay, would you mind waiting here while I check?" She walked off.

"Tony?" The sleepy voice of Brenda called out from the landing above. "Why are you standing outside my door this early on a Saturday morning?"

Tony laughed. "Hey Brenda. Don't you look beautiful.

"You have jokes early in the morning." She yawned as she walked down the stairs. "I bet you don't look that great when you first wake up, either."

Dove had to disagree. She thought he looked perfect. She walked back toward them. "I'm sorry I didn't see your jacket."

"Oh, I put it in my car to bring to the office on Monday." Brenda turned to walk to the table in the foyer. "Let me get my keys. You can get it out the car."

"Thanks, Brenda," Tony said.

Brenda waived his comment off. "Why were you standing outside?"

Dove frowned. "I did that, I'm sorry. I did not know if you wanted me to let him in or not."

Brenda yawned. "Tony can come in anytime, he's harmless."

Dove looked up at Tony wondering if he thought she was being rude. "I'm sorry about that."

"No problem. I could have taken you and made you my sex slave or something... right?"

He flashed a mega-watt smile and she could have sworn the angels began to sing. "Right," she replied thinking that might not be a bad thing. "Umm..." She turned to Brenda as she tapped her Bluetooth that was in her ear. "I'm going to take a run. I'll be back," Dove said as she rushed out the door past Tony.

"Wait," Brenda called after her. "You're going by yourself?"

Dove began stretching as she looked back at Brenda. “Yes, I’ll be fine.”

“I don’t think that’s a good idea. Wait until I get dressed and I will go with you.”

“I will be back before you get dressed. Besides, you will just slow me down.”

“What if someone recognizes you?”

“I’m not worried about that. I’ll see you when I get back.” Dove took off before Brenda could protest more.

Tony watched as the two women took off in different directions.

“Tony, see what direction she goes in while I get my shoes,” Brenda yelled back.

“Alright,” Tony replied, wondering why someone would recognize her and why it concerned Brenda so much. The request to watch Dove run wasn’t needed. He couldn’t take his eyes off her black sweats that hung low on her slim waist as she ran down the block towards the corner. What he wouldn’t give to take his run with her. He could hear Brenda in the background rummaging around before she returned, scrambling around as she vented. “Dove knows she cannot do things like this.”

“She’s just running, Brenda. I don’t think that can kill her.”

“It could if someone recognizes her. Let’s not forget the media crap we’ll have to deal with.”

“What?” Tony asked, confused by the statement.

“People tend to go a little crazy when they see her in person and I like to keep my connection with her on the down low. That way she can always feel safe coming here,” she yelled from the house.

“I must be missing something,” Tony said as he shook his head. “You want me to shadow her?”

Brenda came back to the door half dressed, then looked him up and down. "You are dressed for a run. Would you mind?"

"No." Tony took off jogging before she could change her mind. "I'll grab my jacket when we get back."

"Thanks Tony," he heard her yell as he took chase after Dove. She sounded relieved he thought as he turned the corner.

Dove was half way up the block. Her pace was slow but steady. Tony increased his pace just enough to catch her once she reached the corner.

"Hey there," he said as he jogged in place waiting for traffic to clear.

Her head snapped up. He caught a glance of fear in her eyes, but it disappeared the moment she took him in. He wondered what that was about.

"Hey, again." She hit the button on her Bluetooth, pausing her music.

"Brenda asked me to join you for your run. I hope you don't mind."

"No. Are you a regular runner?"

"A few miles each morning when I can get it in. You?"

"Yes, it clears mind for the day."

"What are you listening to?"

"A playlist I put together."

"Share it with me."

"You're sure?"

"Why not." He shrugged. "It'll give me an idea of what your taste in music."

She laughed as she pushed a few buttons. The traffic cleared and they crossed the street.

"When I'm at Brenda's I usually run to the park. Hit the track for two miles, then run back to the house. Can you handle that?"

They were now at the entrance to the park. "Your turf. I'll follow your lead."

"Keep with the pace of the music," she said as she smiled up at him. "You'll know when to speed up."

He pulled his top sweatshirt off, dropping it on the bench, revealing a white tank top. "Three miles." He pulled his Bluetooth from his pocket, placed it in his ear then turned it on. A song he had never heard began with a nice mellow beat. He began stretching. "Warm up music."

She began jogging in place. "It'll pick up." She gave him a smooth side eye glance then began running.

He watched her for a minute, then looked to the heavens. "Please let the music distract me from looking at that woman's behind." He then followed her around the track.

His prayer was answered. The music began with a nice slow pace. Each song picking up the rhythm one right after the other. By the time they finished the last lap around the track, the music was slowing back to a more relaxed jog. They were back at the bench twenty minutes later. She was jogging in place in front of him as he recovered his top sweatshirt. He tied the sleeves around his neck as he watched her skin glisten from her sweat. How he would like to absorb that moisture with his body.

"A two-mile run in twenty minutes." He shrugged. "Not a bad workout."

She was now jogging backwards as if to put distance between them. "Yes, the heat from your body running next to me gave me the motivation I needed to keep pushing forward."

"Is that a fact?" He stepped towards her. "Your body was my motivation to keep up."

"Is that so?" she asked still jogging backwards.

He saw the bicyclist coming full speed towards her. He reached out and grabbed her, holding her body firmly against his as the cyclist rode by.

"Whoa!" he yelled at the young man's back. "Are you okay?" He stared down at her. Neither making a move to separate.

"Yes." Her voice sounded husky as she stared up at him. "My shield of armor," she joked.

"I could be that," Tony replied trying to calm the roaring sound of his blood rushing through his body. It didn't help that he could feel her heart pounding against his chest. "If you keep looking at me like that I may be tempted to kiss you."

"Okay," she breathlessly replied. He watched as the realization of what he said sank in. She quickly stepped back, looked around then started jogging again. "I guess we better get back."

Tony took in a deep breath. "Yep, I need a cold shower right about now."

She looked over her shoulder grinning "You're going to need more than a cold shower to wash me away."

"It'll do... for now." He jogged behind her.

CHAPTER EIGHT

Brenda and Dove stood on the porch waving as Tony drove away. Frustrated and angry at the way Dove took off, Brenda sat on the stoop determined to set her cousin straight on a few things. She understood Dove still felt she could have a normal life, but with her popularity, her life will never be normal again. There were boundaries Dove had to understand whether she liked them or not. Going out by herself could cause issues and Brenda was not in the mood for one of those events that take place when people find out Dove is in town.

"Don't pull that again, Dove. It's not like before. You know what we have to go through when you're in town. This is not new to you."

"Come on, who would recognize me in this. I have on a cap, sweats, and sneakers. No one even looked my way."

Brenda sighed as Dove sat on the porch beside her. "You know I love you and you know I'm there for whatever. But I think you need to lay low. Take some time to think about your next step without TAT, then move forward. I know you are disappointed with what happened. But I'm sure Aunt Lark and KJ are taking care of things. With time, you will get over TAT."

"I'm so over TAT. I mean we are contractually obligated to do one more tour together. But other than that, I don't need to ever see him again."

Brenda was a little surprised to hear Dove's thoughts on TAT. Her cousin wasn't a casual person when it came to relationships. She thought things were a little more serious between them than what Dove was indicating. "Have you heard from him since you left Atlanta?"

Dove hesitated then replied, "A few text messages."

"Asking you to come back to him?"

"No, not really. He wants me to sign with his label."

"Are you considering leaving KJ?"

"No, KJ is too good to me." She hesitated. "Did you read the new contract from him?"

"Yes, I did and I believe with a few adjustments and the right person presenting them to KJ it would be a great deal for you."

"You're a lawyer. Why can't you do it?"

"You always put me in the middle of you and Aunt Lark. It's time for you to stand up to your mom. It's not like before, you are grown now. You have a say in what you want to do with your career. Put controls in place that will allow you some say in final decisions. Your dad will back you even if your mom will not want to relinquish control. Just speak up for yourself or get someone that will speak on your behalf."

Dove hesitated. "I want to, but I also like the comfort of knowing Mom and Dad are there." She sighed as she sat back on her elbows. "Why can't I have a boring normal life like yours? No contracts, no managers, just a regular nine to five that I love."

Brenda laughed. "Thanks, cuz."

Dove laughed. "I mean, seriously, what ever happened to our biggest problem being what to wear to the high school prom? Or who was getting busy behind the bleachers at the football games, who got to lead the cheers at the basketball games, you know the things normal people do. I don't get to have a boyfriend or a real man in my life without cameras and cell phones in my face. Sometimes, I wonder if singing is worth it."

"Well, the games weren't all that. We lost most of them, football and basketball. The prom was a joke. I have pictures to prove it. And as for men, well I don't have one of them either. So, what's your point?"

Dove laughed. "You have Timothy."

"No, I don't. Tim is a player. He's a good stiff one when I need it. You get to travel and meet people we just dream about. You can't tell me you don't get a rush when people recognize you and want to be near you or pay money to hear you sing. You come to life behind a microphone. Belle St. Clair, the star." She laughed.

"It's a persona. A well-rehearsed stage act. People think life on the road is glamorous, and there are parties all the time. Well, as KJ taught me, to be good it's hard work. You have to keep your body in shape, your voice fresh and perform with people, some you really don't like."

"You love every minute of it."

Dove looked at Brenda and smiled. "I do. But there has to be a way to have what my mom and dad have and the music, you know."

Brenda laughed. "That part is up to you, Dove. You have to balance the professional life with the private life. Your mom really controlled this first deal based on what Grandma Sparrow wanted for her life. Aunt Lark turned away from that. Now she is trying to make up for not fulfilling her mother's dreams for her through you. You will be twenty-one, soon. It's up to you to balance your career in a way that will allow you to fulfill your dream, not someone else's. If Grandma Sparrow's dream to sing at an inauguration is what you want to follow, then go for it. If you want the life of Bey and Whit, then go for that. You are now in control. Take this opportunity to do what you love, but remember to take some time for you." Brenda looked up to the sky. "God gave you a beautiful voice that brings people joy. You don't let something like that go without sharing it."

"And a man who I can love and who will love me for who I am, how do I find that?"

"How did you find TAT?"

Dove looked at her cousin whom she trusted more than anyone in the world. Brenda was the only person she would even consider telling about TAT's messages. "It wasn't all of that. It ended with him sending me hateful messages."

"What did they say?"

Dove hesitated. Would Brenda ask her to leave her home if she knew of TAT's threats? Being an officer of the court, would she be compelled to take action, get the police involved? That would lead to more publicity that she did not need. But not telling her could put her in danger. At least she would know to stay on alert. She pulled her cell phone from her pocket, put her code in, then shared the messages with Brenda.

After a few moments of silence, during which time Dove assumed Brenda was reading the messages, she spoke. "I need you to keep them to yourself."

"These are direct threats on your person, Dove. Did you tell your parents about this?"

Dove shook her head. "Who says that?"

"What?"

"Direct threat on your person."

"A person who works in a court of law and recognizes threats when she reads them. Now answer the question. Did you tell your parents or anyone about these messages?"

"No. They will only worry."

"As they should," Brenda replied in a tone that was no longer her cousin, but that calm matter-of-fact tone she always used in court.

She turned to look at Brenda. "Imagine the publicity that will result in me releasing those messages to the authorities. Do you think I will have a chance at the career I want?"

"You would have a life of not looking over your shoulder."

Dove stood, wiping her pants from sitting on the porch. "It's been a few days since I've heard from him." Trying her best not to show any concern for the situation, she changed the subject. "Do you think my butt is getting big?"

Brenda gave her an incredulous look. "You should ask Tony. He was watching it while you were running."

That statement knocked all thoughts of TAT right out the window. "I was watching his too." She grinned. "Do you really think chocolate yum yum was checking me out?"

"If you are referring to my boss," Brenda laughed. "Yes, chocolate yum yum was checking you out."

Dove's frown turned into a bright smile. "We did have a moment when we were running."

"You... and Tony?" Brenda speculated.

"He is a fine man. Why haven't you grabbed that?"

"Well, for one, he's my boss. I can't get busy with my boss and two, Tony's someone I look up to. He is smart, not just in the courtroom, but he has a little street in him that most people in our profession only think they have."

"Is he married?" She caught Brenda's frown. "I'm just asking."

Brenda stood and turned to walk into the house. "No." She opened the door, looked back at her cousin and said, "But he is also not a booty call kind of guy, even for a stage thot like you. Then she ran into the house."

Dove ran in behind her. "No, you didn't just call me a thot."

♩♩♩

"Fazi, it's Pete. I'm on the parents' house. Both are inside."

"Any sign of the chick?"

"Not so far."

"Sit tight. She's bound to show up at some point."

"You got it. I'll check in when I have something to report."

CHAPTER NINE

Monday morning Tony was leaving court when he received a message to call Steve Andersen, an ADA in the county where he once worked. He maintained a very good working relationship with many of the ADAs there. Steve and Tony were close. He was probably calling to have drinks after work. He stepped inside one of the empty interview rooms in the courthouse and returned the call. His assumption was wrong.

It all seemed like it was just yesterday when Jason came home during his second year at college and said his girlfriend from high school, Shaniqua was pregnant. He decided to leave school to get a full-time job to support his child. That was the way Elaine raised her children. They were all taught to take responsibility for their actions. If you get a girl pregnant you be a man, step up to the plate and do the right thing. Don't expect that baby's momma to do it all by herself. That's exactly what Jason did. He started a position with the local school system and was doing well. Jason was taking night classes to finish his degree; working during the day and spent his weekends with Jasmine. Jason and Shaniqua stopped seeing each other, but Jason would go every Friday, after work, to the project Shaniqua lived in to give her a child support check and pick up Jasmine. It was on a Friday night that Jason went to pick up Jasmine when he was walking back to the car holding Jasmines hand when shots rang out. Jason threw Jasmine to the ground and covered her with his body. He protected his child, but lost his life. Jasmine's mother wasn't willing to raise his niece on her own. As most families do, his mother took custody of the child. Tony helped with the custody papers of the then eight-year-old and had helped with raising the child who was now sixteen and in high school.

According to Steve, a parent was in his office attempting to get an arrest warrant for Jasmine Perry, and the address given was his mother's address. Steve recognized the name and knew it was Tony's niece. He took the report and advised the parent he would be in touch with them once the investigation was complete. It was clear to Steve, the parent was very adamant about the action they wanted the DA's office to take. When Steve told him what Jasmine did, Tony laughed and asked if he was serious. When Steve replied he was, Tony sobered. Steve agreed to meet him at his mom's house to take Jasmine's statement. Tony called his office to advise he would be out for the remainder of the afternoon then headed in the direction of his mother's house.

Tony, Elaine and Steve were seated at the kitchen table when Jasmine came into the room. Tony's expression showed his anger. Before Jasmine took a seat, she kissed Tony on the cheek.

"That's not going to work this time Jasmine. I want you to tell me everything that happened."

"Uncle Tony, I told Susan two weeks ago that when she brushes her hair in class, it keeps falling on my clothes. I'd be walking around school all day long like a dog shed on me or something. All she had to do was brush her hair in the restroom like everybody else does. No, she got to sit there in front of my desk and brush it knowing full well that blonde stuff keeps falling on me. I told her yesterday if she did it again today, I was going to cut it off. And I wore my black cashmere sweater you brought me. I didn't want that blonde hair on my new sweater. And, Uncle Tony, you told me to always keep my word, so I did. When she brushed her hair in front of me today I told Mrs. Carter I was going to cut Susan's hair and why and did it."

Jasmine told the story so fast that it took Tony and Steve a minute to catch on to what she said. The only way they knew the story was complete was the fact that she crossed her arms at her chest and sighed heavily. Steve was the first to crack a smile, while Tony sat there and stared at his niece. He wanted to let go and laugh but knew that would not help matters any.

Tony turned to Steve. "May I see you on the porch for a minute."

When the two stepped out the door they ventured further into the yard, then exploded into laughter.

Once they composed themselves Steve spoke first. "I'll play bad cop, you be good cop this time."

Tony looked at his friend Steve and wondered if he would instill the fear of God into Jasmine. Steve stood six two and weighed in around 220 with steel blue eyes that bent the knees of some criminals.

"I want you to frighten her, but would you be nice about it, this is my sixteen-year-old niece?" Tony asked.

"The issue is not getting Jasmine in line, the problem is going to be the parents. Their hazel eyed daughter's beautiful blonde hair is gone." Steve imitated the mother. "And when I made the comment, it will grow back, she went into a fit stating that wasn't the point. She feels those heathens need to be taught a lesson on how to deal with conflict in a civilized environment."

Tony's eyes narrowed. "Were those her exact words?" he asked.

"Verbatim." Steve raised his eyebrows making sure Tony got his message. "You knew when you purchased this house for your mother, in this district Jasmine was going to encounter situations like this."

"Jasmine is a smart girl. She deserves the best education I can provide just as this girl Susan does."

"I agree." Steve nodded. "However, the climate is changing from when you and I were in school. The 'elites' as they believe they are, have become bolder in their position of privilege. They now believe it is their birthright to establish dominance over any and all who are different from them."

Tony knew what Steve was not saying. He wasn't willing to bow to the so-called elites nor would he instruct Jasmine to do so. "Set up a meeting with the parents, the girl, the teacher and the principal for tomorrow. I'll handle the parents. You handle Jasmine."

"Give me another minute to gather myself." Steve laughed. "I can't believe she cut the girl's hair. Truth be told, I probably would have done worse."

Tony took one look at Steve and joined him in the laughter. "Hell, I did worse."

The two looked at each other and burst into laughter as they shouted, "The super glue."

"Man, I never laughed so hard in my life." Steve was now bent over trying to compose himself.

"Hey, I told the man to ease up," Tony attempted to explain his actions. "He kept with the pranks."

"You were the new kid on the block, Tony. Hell, we had to do something to have fun in the office."

"Hiding my case files was not the answer. I took my job seriously."

"I know, man, but putting superglue in Reggie's chair." He laughed again. "I keep seeing him trying to climb out of his pants while they were still glued to the chair. That was just too much. Remind me to never get on your bad side."

"Hey, I think I'm a pretty decent guy, just don't cross me," Tony said with a shrug of his shoulder.

"Admit it. You were pissed because the man said you were too wound up and needed a woman. And he was right."

Tony shook his head. "Yes, he was right at the time. That didn't make it his business to say it."

"You were pulling long hours and making all of us look bad. Hell, you probably still do. When was the last time you went out?"

"Friday night?"

"Your mother's house don't count," Steve taunted. "When was the last time you were with a woman? Stephanie?"

Tony shrugged off the question.

"Look, with the craziness we deal with in the court system, you need an escape. Someone can take your mind from the evil we see. Someone to make you see that sweet side of life. You know."

"That's the price we pay for keeping the streets safe," Tony replied with a nod of his head. "Speaking of which, let's get this niece of mine straight before she ends up with an unnecessary juvie record."

"You got it," Steve agreed then walked back towards the house.

Dove's face appeared in Tony's mind as he followed Steve inside.

On his drive home, Tony turned on the music in his car. The soulful sound of Belle St. Clair drifted through the speakers. Thoughts of his conversation with Steve came to mind. They did deal with low lifes in court. If one wasn't careful, the evil they saw would become the norm. It was important to find a decompressor once they were outside the courthouse. He had his family, his mother, his sister, niece and nephews. But he did not have the one person to share his day with. He had not met the woman he could imagine coming home to every day, telling her the horrors or the victories of his profession. Having someone there to ease the sting of disappointment with the system. Having someone to love the hurt away and give him the strength to go in and try again another day. Dove's face filled his mind again.

He chuckled to himself. "I wouldn't have a problem waking up to Dove in my arms every morning."

Friday night, it felt like an angel falling from heaven falling into his arms. Just the thought of her touch sent shivers through his body. She was the reason he stopped by Brenda's house the next day. He wanted to see Dove again, just to make sure he wasn't dreaming she existed. There was no mistaking her interest in him, or his reaction to her in the park. A spark was definitely there. Tony was never a shy man and always approached women with ease and confidence, but there was something about Dove. The conflicting messages in his brain caused him to be cautious. There was something about her that wasn't clear. A hidden factor under all that beauty. The vision of her body running Saturday morning sent the 'danger zone' signal through his brain. However, his body was indicating go forth and concur. It was strange, the possessiveness he felt towards a woman he didn't really know. Yet, for some strange reason he felt he knew her, but that couldn't be. Friday night was his first time ever laying eyes on her... or was it.

The horn from a vehicle behind him brought him back to the present. Tony put his hand up as a gesture of apology to the motorist behind him and pulled off through the green light and headed home.

CHAPTER TEN

Tuesday morning, as all parties involved sat around the conference room at the high school, Tony observed Susan, the young woman at the center of the dispute. Her hair was now styled in a short bob with highlights, which gave her a very mature look. But the most prominent feature in the young girl was an air of superiority.

The principal began the meeting introducing everyone including Steve as the prosecutor from Henrico County and Tony as the attorney representing Jasmine. The principal asked Susan's parents if they would like to have an attorney present and they declined indicating their daughter was the victim. The principal explained the situation and turned the questioning over to Steve.

Steve questioned Susan and she gave a heart-wrenching tear producing version of the events. He then asked Jasmine to explain what took place and she described the events leading up to the incident with her normal flair minus the rolling of the neck.

"There, she admitted to cutting my daughters hair," Mrs. Defazio declared. "Case closed. I want her expelled and charges filed."

The principal than turned to Tony. "Mr. Perry, do you have any questions?"

"Just a few." Tony nodded, looked at Susan and smiled. "My apologies for your loss, Susan. I must say your hair is very becoming on you."

"That's not the issue," the mother interjected.

"You are correct, it's not. The issue is why did Jasmine resort to such drastic measures," Tony replied with an edge then turned back to the young girl. "Susan, did Jasmine ever talk with you about combing your hair in class?"

"I don't know, maybe." The nonchalant attitude filled the air.

"Did she or didn't she?"

"Yes." Susan smirked.

"In retaliation you and your friend-" He looked at his notes. "Kerri took Jasmine's clothes and hid them during gym then locked her in the steam room turning the temperature to high. Is that correct?"

"Maybe."

"It is or it isn't."

Susan rolled her eyes. "Yes, but that still didn't give the bitch the right to cut my hair."

"Watch your language," the principal interjected. "Please continue, Mr. Perry."

"Did it occur to you, turning up the heat and locking her in could have damaged her skin or caused health issues?"

"She's an African. I figured she would be used to the heat." Susan smirked.

Tony looked around the room at the administrators. "I'll just let that sit in the air for consumption." He turned back to Susan. "You and your friends are pretty popular. So, tell me why, Susan, why is it that Kerri or the other classmates didn't warn you what was happening?" He shrugged. "Jasmine had to apply pressure to cut your hair, yet you didn't feel it nor did anyone warn you... why?"

"Well..." Susan shrugged. "I don't know."

"All right. Tell me exactly what Kerri was doing."

"Well, Kerri was holding my arms showing me where she was going to put her tattoo."

"Let me make sure I have the scene right. Kerri was holding your arms talking while she and others in the class watched Jasmine cut your hair?"

"Yeah," Susan replied looking around at the people in the room.

Tony looked at the mother, then at the teacher, then the principal. "Could someone explain to me why Kerri or the other students are not her being persecuted along with Jasmine?" He then caught Mr. Defazio's eye. Tony could see the father knew where he was going with his line of questions. "Can anyone tell me why Susan was not charged when Jasmine was locked in the sauna?" Tony shook his head then turned to the teacher. "Ms. Tate, teaching is a hard job and I commend you for all you do. But I must ask, did Jasmine complain to you about Susan brushing her hair in class?"

Ms. Tate cleared her throat "Yes, she has and I have spoken to Susan on several occasions about it."

Tony continued, "Did Susan make adjustments on those things when asked?"

"No," Ms. Tate replied.

"I don't see the point to any of these questions," Mrs. Defazio stated. "The fact remains, she cut Susan's hair and needs to be taught a lesson on how to handle conflict in a civilized manner."

"I agree a lesson needs to be learned here by both Susan and Jasmine. From what I've heard, it seems Jasmine took steps to resolve the conflict before it escalated. She spoke with Susan and the authority in that classroom. Susan chose to ignore Jasmine and Ms. Tate. I contend that it was Susan who infringed on Jasmine's rights. It was Susan's actions that led to the incident."

"I did no such thing," Susan shouted. "That baboon cut my hair for no reason."

"Susan," Mrs. Clarke shouted. "You apologize for that right now."

"You will not force my daughter to apologize to... her," Mrs. Defazio squeaked.

Tony held up his hand. "No need. Please know, I am not condoning Jasmine's actions in any way. However, I will not allow you to rest the entire blame for this incident on her shoulders. Susan shall bear a portion of this blame, as will the administration. Once this issue was reported, it became the responsibility of the administration to prevent it from going any further. Not holding Susan or Kerri accountable for their actions, but insisting on holding Jasmine accountable for hers can be viewed as discrimination. Do we want to pursue this in a court of law?" His eyes went to the principal.

"How dare you sit there and put this on us, it was my daughter that was wronged," the mother yelled.

The mother glared at Steve, then turned to the husband, who remain silent during the entire proceedings. "Say something, don't just sit there."

Mr. Defazio glared at Tony, nodded his head then turned to his wife and stood. "I believe it would be in Susan's best interest to let this issue drop. Jasmine, please accept my apology on Susan's behalf for her behavior towards you." He turned away from his wife who was spitting mad at his response. "Ms. Tate, I would like a moment to speak with you in private."

"But Daddy..." Susan began.

Her father stopped her words with one look. "Now, Susan." He held his hand out to Tony. "Thank you for insisting we meet here. You would have won this if it had gone to court. I owe you one."

As the door closed, Steve turned to Tony. "I think you may have a friend for life. Did you see that look from the father when you mentioned the sauna incident?"

Tony frowned. "I did. Made me not to want to be on the receiving end. Do you know anything about him?"

"No, never heard of them until now," Steve replied. "What are you going to do about Jasmine?"

"Her behind is mine for the next month," he laughed, gathered his things, then motioned to Jasmine to follow him.

CHAPTER ELEVEN

It was close to lunchtime when Tony arrived back at his office. He stopped by the deli next door and picked up a sandwich. His plan was to eat lunch at his desk and catch up on whatever he missed that morning. With briefcase in one hand, sandwich and drink in the other, he turned the knob, then turned and pushed the door opened with his back. He stepped inside allowing the door to swing close. He looked up and froze.

"Hi."

The smile was instantaneous and it flowed from his head to his toes as the woman who disturbed his sleep for the last two nights materialized.

"Hello," he said standing in the middle of the floor with his hands filled with items.

"Brenda was called away and said I should wait here for her." Dove took the sandwich bag and drink from his hand then placed them on the desk. "I hope that's okay."

Dressed in a pair of jeans, a midriff top, a ball cap, ponytail hanging out the back and sunshades she had him lost for words. It took him a moment to clear his brain enough to respond.

"Of course."

"She wasn't sure where you were, but didn't think you'd mind if I hid out here."

Finally able to move, Tony sat his briefcase on his desk. "I don't mind."

They stood there staring at each other for a long somewhat comfortable moment. "Is this your daughter?"

She was pointing to a picture on his bookshelf of Jasmine in one of her dance troop outfits.

"My niece, Jasmine. She loves to dance."

She pointed to another picture. "Girlfriend and sons?"

Tony laughed. "No, umm, that's my sister and her sons."

She smiled as she turned back towards him. "You seem to have a lot of pictures of your family."

"They are the reason I do what I do."

"You keep your motivation front and center. I do the same," she said while pulling a locket from under her top. She opened it and held it out to him. "This is my grandmother. She's my inspiration."

He leaned across the desk taking the trinket in his hands. He could feel the heat from her body as he held it in his hand. The instant rush of blood resulted yet again at her nearness. "She's a beautiful woman."

"Yes, she is," Dove agreed. "She's the reason I do what I do."

Tony nodded in understanding as he felt the loss of her nearness the moment she stepped back. Having no idea what she did for a living, he replied, "I'm certain she is very proud of you."

She shrugged. "She would be upset over the mess I've made of things."

Not sure why, but Tony felt he needed to reassure her, of what he had no idea. He pointed to a chair in front of his desk. "It's been my experience that just about anything that's broken can be fixed. All you need is the desire and determination to mend fences." He sat once she was seated.

"Oh, I don't know. Some fences aren't meant to be repaired."

"That may be true. Most of the time it's our doing. We try to keep people in our life longer than God intends."

"Does God have a presence in your life?"

"Very much so and I have the marks on my behind from my mother whenever I think otherwise." Tony laughed. "I'm not your every Sunday in church, Bible toting kind of brother, but I do believe He is present in my life and pray He will always be." He marveled at her smile and how it brightened the room. "What about you?"

"Strongly." She lowered her lashes then looked back at him. "People don't believe that because of my lifestyle, but I know I am blessed because He lives within me."

"You're a church girl." He smiled.

She laughed. "Yes, I grew up in the church."

"Only a church girl would say He lives within me."

"Tipped off by my vernacular."

"I like your vernacular," he said before catching himself.

"The feeling is mutual."

Moments ticked off the clock as they sat there, eyes held until he spoke. "Is it me or do you feel the heat between us?"

"It has been foremost in my mind since Friday." She blushed. "What do you think we should do about that?"

"Hmm, I would be interested in exploring the possibility of you and me. What do you think about that?"

She took in a deep breath. "It's not easy being with a person like me. I come with a lot of baggage."

"What are you? Twenty... twenty-one? It can't be but so much baggage."

"Baggage is measured by life choices, not by years."

Tony nodded, understanding her meaning. "True. Let's eliminate those issues that may interfere with my next move. Are you married?" She shook her head no. "Engaged?" She shook her head again no. "Baby daddy drama?"

She laughed, "No."

"Ah, boyfriend."

"Friend drama."

"Mutual decision or is he having difficulty letting go?" He could see the turmoil in her eyes, just like he saw in the park. She lowered them as if shielding something from him.

"It's a difficult situation."

"One that will prevent you from moving forward with another man who finds you to be irresistible?"

She looked up into his eyes and replied a resounding, "No."

Their gazes held again. Her eyes filling him with an unexplainable desire. "Your eyes are begging me to kiss your lips. Are you prepared for the consequences that may follow?"

"Contrary to public opinion I am not a loose woman, Anthony. I'm looking for love, not just a lover. So, before you make that move to fill the desire in my eyes, be sure you are ready to handle my reaction to your kiss."

Tony stood, walked around his desk, placed his hands on the arm of the chair she was sitting in then leaned in.

"I can handle whatever you bring."

He lowered his head to cover her lips with his. The kiss was what he imagined it would be - sweet, intoxicating and nowhere near enough. He pulled slightly away taking his fill of her beauty and smiled.

"I am so in trouble."

She rubbed her thumb over his lips. "Yes, you are."

She was pulling him in for another kiss when there was a knock on the door that caused him to stand.

"Hey," Brenda said as she opened the door and walked in. "I got caught up with a witness." She sat down in the seat next to Dove. "Sorry about that. Have you eaten lunch?"

Tony walked back behind his desk as Dove smoothly nodded no to her cousin.

Brenda looked from one to the other, then frowned. "Did I interrupt something?"

"No." Dove cleared her throat.

Tony chuckled as he reached for his sandwich. "Lunch, you interrupted my lunch that was once hot but has now gone cold."

Dove laughed. "Allow me to make it up to you. Dinner at Brenda's place, I'll cook?"

"How could I turn down such a tasty offer? What time?"

"Seven?" Dove replied.

Brenda kept looking from one to the other. "Did I miss something?"

Did you ever, Tony thought as he cleared his throat. "I'll see you at seven."

"Did you forget your conference call with the project team tonight?"

Dove closed her eyes and sighed. "I did. We're supposed to go over new tracks tonight."

"That's right." Brenda then added, "And no, you cannot put it off."

Dove looked up at him. Tony could see, tonight would not happen.

"You can cook for me another night. I'm not going anywhere."

The smile she sent his way warmed his heart. He watched as the two women stood to leave. "Be careful with that," he said.

"What?"

"That smile is lethal. I may have to have you detained if you keep that up."

"Pull out the handcuffs, Anthony. You're going to need them." Dove opened the door and walked out leaving Brenda standing there with her mouth wide open.

She turned to Tony. "Are you sure I didn't miss something?"

"Get out," Tony laughed. "I have work to do."

"Don't let the vision of my little cousin's behind distract you." Brenda smirked then walked out the office closing the door behind her.

CHAPTER TWELVE

Wednesday morning Tony went into the office to ensure all court cases for the day were covered and to let his secretary know he would be out part of the morning. There was a tap on his door.

"Come in." He was surprised to look up to find Brenda standing there.

"Hey, Boss, do you have a minute?"

Looking back at the document on his desk he waved her in. "Sure. It's seven-thirty in the morning. I thought your days started at nine."

"Funny," Brenda said as she took a seat in front of his desk. There was a hesitation before she spoke. "Do you mind if I close the door?"

Tony stopped writing and looked up. "No, close it."

He watched as Brenda closed the door then returned to the chair. She took a deep breath.

"What's going on?"

"Dove is in a little bit of a messy situation. I need a level head to give me guidance on how to handle what I know." She took a deep breath. "You may have heard about it. The fight in Atlanta between TAT between KJ Murphy."

The confusion on his face must have been evident. Brenda gave him a you know look. "The rapper TAT and the music producer KJ Murphy."

"I don't know either one of them," Tony confessed. "What do they have to do with Dove?"

Brenda frowned at him. "You never heard of TAT?"

"No."

Brenda laughed, shaking her head. "Not surprising. Let me get the story out then you do you and advise. TAT and Dove had a fight that ended up with KJ stepping in. There were pictures and stories all over the internet claiming the fight between the two men was over Dove. According to reports not only did Dove and TAT split because of said incident, he was arrested for possession of a firearm."

"He's an ex-felon?"

"Yes," Brenda replied then continued. "It has recently come to my attention that he, TAT, has been sending Dove threatening messages. The most violent mentions having her taken out. She's asked me not to take action or mention it to anyone." She exhaled. "I'm an officer of the court and this is my cousin whom I love dearly. And to be honest I don't think sitting back and hoping this situation will disappear is the way to go." She stopped and looked up at him. "Should I step in to encourage her to take some action against him or keep my promise to remain quiet?"

Tony sat back trying to gather the facts as they were presented without losing his cool. The fact that his skin was crawling from the information had to be put on hold. "Dove's boyfriend is a rapper named TAT."

"Ex-boyfriend."

"Okay, ex-boyfriend. They had a disagreement and someone name KJ intervened. There are stories about the incident on the internet. Since that time, he has sent threatening messages to Dove. She shared them with you and asked that you not take any action legal action against him. Is that about right?"

"Yes. But there's more." She sat closer to the desk as if revealing a secret. "TAT has been pressuring Dove to sign a contract with his label but Dove doesn't want to leave KJ. So, I did some research into this label TAT is involved with and they are some shady people. They not only want, but need a talent like Dove to get the label to a point where they can compete with someone like KJ. According to my sources in Atlanta, this isn't the first time they attempted to use coercion to get people to sign with them. The last person that signed with them did so under duress. His family was threatened when he refused to sign with them. He didn't and his six-year-old daughter went missing. The next day he signed the contract and he found her in his backyard that evening. Now he is locked into a five-year entertainment deal with them."

Tony was more confused than ever. He sat up and released a chuckle. "Okay," he started. "Dove is a singer?"

Brenda gave him the most incredulous look he had ever seen. "Tony...do you listen to the radio, watch television, look at music award shows?"

"Not really." He shook his head. "What does that have to do with Dove?"

"You don't know who Dove is?"

"She's your cousin."

Brenda began to laugh. "You saw her at my house. You went running with her and y'all was doing some freaking googly eyed stuff sitting right here in your office and you don't know who she is?"

"She's a beautiful woman who I enjoy being around."

"Yes, well she calls you chocolate yum yum. I guess the feeling is mutual."

Tony broke out into a huge grin. He had to catch himself from jumping up. "Did she say anything else about me?"

"What is this high school? You want me to take a note home with me?" Brenda teased from frustration more than anything else. She held out her hand. "Give me the remote to your television."

Tony opened his center desk drawer reached in and handed her the remote. Curious to see what she was up to, he turned towards the monitor on the wall as Brenda switched to a music channel. She did a search for Belle St. Clair. "I have some of her music. She has a soulful voice."

Brenda turned to him. "Have you ever watched some of her videos?"

"Can't say that I have."

"Then you should get a hell of a kick out of this."

She pushed play on the remote and Tony was stunned to see Dove walking down the street looking around singing one of his favorite songs, Driven, the single from her first CD. The woman was wearing a red flowing dress, heels that made her legs look long and her hair swinging around her shoulders. With all of that, he could clearly see it was Dove. He couldn't believe the sexy vixen strutting down the street in the video was Dove... his Dove. But it was. That was the same woman who fell into his arms just four nights ago. The same woman he kissed right in this office on yesterday.

"Belle is Dove?" he asked unbelieving his own words.

Brenda placed the remote on his desk. "Yes. And she's in trouble."

Tony picked up the remote, paused the video. "Tell me what the messages said exactly."

"The last one stated he would be in touch with her soon and if she didn't sign the contract he would have her taken out."

"Anything against her family or you?"

"No, just her."

"You need to put security on her." He pulled out a legal pad and a pen and gave it to Brenda. "I want this TAT's legal name, where he lives and the name of the label he is trying to force Dove to sign. Also, I want copies of every text message he has sent her."

"What are you going to do?"

"What you should have done, have him arrested for threatening to murder her."

"Wait, Tony, it's not as simple as arresting him."

"She is not an average citizen. Anything she does will be in the media before the ink dries. Once the media gets wind of this, it will impact her career. His people will start a smear campaign that could ruin her.

"Is there?"

"Is there what?"

"Anything going on between her and this KJ person?"

"No. He's old enough to be her father," Brenda declared "The point is these people fight dirty. Neither Dove or her parents are prepared to go up against them. The only reason things are dying down now is because of KJ Murphy."

"Who is he again?"

Brenda threw up her hands in frustration. "He's a music producer. He has written and produced songs for every big name normal people know."

"And he has Dove on his list to produce?"

"Yes, he did her first CD and is working on the next with her. He and my Aunt Lark are old friends.

He had taken Dove under his wing for the last three years. The only misstep so far has been TAT."

Tony sat back and sighed. "Brenda, I'm a firm believer that the best way to handle street is to get in their face." She raised an eyebrow and he laughed. "Yes, I may be lost in the music category, but I do have a little street in me. Where is Dove now?"

"She's at my house going over her contract with KJ Music with her mother."

"Let's get over there." Tony stood gathering his things. "I think this may be easier to handle than you know."

"As a man who is infatuated with her or as a DA?"

Tony had to think on that for a moment. "Look, Brenda, I'm not going to lie. Dove has me more than a little mesmerized. She got a little piece of me. I don't know how or when it happened, but it has. Am I pissed because neither of you told me who she was... yeah. But before I deal with that, I need to ensure she is safe."

"Okay," Brenda agreed. "But that not knowing who she is, that's on you. Every man walking the earth with blood running through his veins knows who Belle St. Clair is."

♩♩♩

"Fazi, hit pay dirt," Pete boasted. "I have Belle St. Clair in my eye sight. Followed her mother to a house on the North side. What do you want me to do?"

"Stay on her until I get further instructions."

Fazi disconnected the call then made another. "Joe, Fazi in Richmond. We have Belle St. Clair in our sights. What do you want us to do?"

"Send me the info. I'll pass it on to the client."

CHAPTER THIRTEEN

This is it, Dove thought as she watched her mother step out of the car. The conference call with KJ was scheduled for eleven that morning. That gave her an hour to get her mother to understand what she wanted from this contract before the call. The two of them could be over powering, so Dove knew she had to be prepared with her main points. She had discussed them with her father and knew he was available for back up if she needed him. But this was something she was determined to do for herself.

In two months, she would be twenty-one years old. Brenda was right, it was time to put on the big girl panties and take control of her life. That included cleaning up the mess with TAT and opening the door of possibilities with Anthony. The thought brought a smile to her face as she opened the door for her mother.

"Hello, Mother." Dove stepped onto the porch and hugged Lark, then took her briefcase from her hand. The two walked into the house arm in arm.

"How are you today?" Lark held her daughter tight. "Any word from TAT?"

"Some." Dove placed the briefcase on the table in the kitchen. "I made us some tea. Would you like some?"

"Of course," Lark replied as she took a seat at the table.

Dove placed a cup of tea in front of her mother then sat across from her with her own cup in her hand.

"Mother, how did you know Dad was the one?"

A slight frown appeared on her mother's face, which caused Dove to smile. "He told me so." Then she laughed.

Dove joined in. "Really?"

"Really." She lowered her head and smiled. "People are amazed when I tell them things about your father. Everyone thinks because he's quiet that I'm the one who wears the pants in the house."

She smiled. "Well, truth be told I would walk on water if that man told me to."

Dove giggled like a little girl, causing her mother to look up at her.

"You've met someone?" Lark asked.

Dove sat her cup down and smiled up at her mother. "His name is Anthony Perry. He's Brenda's boss." She frowned. "I'm not sure how she is going to react to that." She closed her eyes and sighed. "But I like him, Mother." She then looked up. "There's this feeling I get whenever I'm in a room with him." She shrugged her shoulders. "I just tingle all over." She laughed. "He's so intelligent. And so different from the men I meet in the industry. He reminds me of Dad in a way. Anthony appears to be all serious and starchy, but he's funny and caring and..."

"Fine," Lark suggested.

Dove laughed. "Oh, my goodness, Mother, he is so fine and has a hardcore body to boot. He just does it for me, you know what I mean?"

"I have an idea." Lark reached across the table and captured her hand. "You're in love?"

"I don't know but I'm certainly in deep, deep, deep like." She froze. "Wait, I have to write that down." She jumped up and grabbed her tablet, made a note then sat back down.

"Music comes to mind when you think of him?" Lark asked.

"Yes, isn't that crazy?"

"No." Her mother shook her head. "When a man makes your heart sing, you'll know that's the right one. That's what your grandmother used to tell me."

Dove smiled. "Anthony does that." She nodded. "He makes one or two other things sing too. You know what I mean."

"I have an idea, yes." Lark blushed. "What about TAT? That situation with him was only a month ago. Are you over him?"

"I was never that much into TAT." She shook her head. "When I think of Anthony, I can see you and Dad."

Her mother sat back and smiled. She could see tears on the brink of falling from her eyes.

"What is it, Mother," Dove asked in a concerned voice.

Her mother shook her head as if trying to compose herself. "Parents wonder if they are setting the right example for their children. Mother's love for Daddy always made me look for it in the men I was with. I'm very proud to see that trait is in you. You're looking for love, not just a lover."

Dove smiled. "I said that very thing recently."

They both looked at each other and laughed. "I guess Mother's words are instilled in us." Lark sighed. "So, when do I get meet this Anthony?"

"It's fresh, but I don't think it will be too long." Dove took a sip of tea. "Now, let's talk about our call with Mr. Murphy. There are a few things I need you to request on my behalf."

"Okay, but I want to discuss something with you before we begin." her mother said as she pulled her computer from her briefcase. "I think it's time for you to seek professional representation. I'm your mother and knew enough to work with Kenneth on your first contract. But, this next one is going to set you for life. You father and I believe you need someone who has an extensive background in the entertainment industry."

Dove sat back and smiled as her mother spoke. He worked his magic, she thought as her mother continued. The points she was hearing were exactly the ones she had discussed with her dad.

"The last point I want to make is concerning your grandmother. You and I know what her dream was. You are going to be an "A" lister. I feel it in my heart. In no way do I want you to put your dreams aside for your grandmother or me. All I ask of you is if the opportunity presents itself, please consider fulfilling that dream."

Dove read the document and smiled a sigh of relief. "I promise."

♩♩♩

On a conference call with KJ, Dove listened as her mother negotiated the changes Dove was requesting. She listened intently at the pros and cons of what she considered simple changes to the contract. She wasn't asking for outrageous money, in fact royalties and secondary income from the deal was more than acceptable.

The hitch seemed to be over the number of tours and appearances for the next five years. Dove thought the number of CD releases for that time period was aggressive, but certainly doable. Since her first CD went platinum and broke a few records, the anticipation of the second and third CDs going double platinum was on everyone's mind. Lark used that to introduce the exclusive deal allowing Dove to have final say on performing with other artists. The second stipulation was if for any reason KJ Music goes under or is sold to another entity, Dove will exercise her right to part ways with the company. In addition, if Kenneth "KJ" Murphy separates association from KJ Music, said option will also be at Dove's discretion. As the two professionals continued with their argument, Dove's mind drifted. All the terms meant a lot of time and dedication from her. How would she balance it all? She wanted what her parents had—the big house with the white picket fence wasn't necessary, but a nice home with someone who loved her for her would be nice. She closed her eyes when the image of Anthony filled her mind.

"Dove, are you listening?" her mother asked. "What about the summer tour? You are under contract. "

"Yes, yes I'm listening. Is TAT still a on the roster?" No one replied. "I'll take that as a yes."

"Yes, he is," KJ replied. "You will have to perform with him. You've been in this business long enough to know there is an ugly side to the music business. There will always be people like TAT around. He's arrogant and a showboat, that's why he pulls in the crowds. None of the sponsors are pulling him from the tour at this point. "

"But they don't mind pulling me?"

"Dove, no one wants to pull either of you. The sponsors want both. I know how you feel about the incident."

"It's not just the one incident, Mr. Murphy," Dove stated. "It's his insistence that I sign with his label."

"There is no way I will let that happen. As for the concert tour, sponsors could sue for damages if you pull out. You and KJ music will be liable."

"I'm going to hold off on any decision regarding the summer tour," Lark declared. "Dove's new reps will deal with that decision as soon as they are on board."

"There's a lot invested in this tour, Dove, " KJ exclaimed.

"I understand that, Kenneth," Lark spoke. "None of it more valuable than my daughter's well-being.

"We're not that far apart on closing this deal," KJ acknowledged. "I'll have my reps review the clause as well. If we can find anything TAT did was illegal at any of the previous concerts that Dove was a party to, we may have something to go on."

The front door opened. Dove looked at the clock, Brenda should be at work, she thought, then turned to her mother and whispered, "You keep talking, I'll check the door."

She walked into the living room and looked over the bannister.

"Hey," Brenda spoke. "Tony is with me. Are you decent?"

Dove smiled. "Yes, yes, of course."

Tony walked in and followed Brenda up the stairs to the main landing.

"Hi." She smiled, then noticed there was something a little different in his demeanor.

"I think you and I need to talk," Tony said then turned to Brenda. "You have somewhere we can talk?"

"Sure, you can go downstairs," Brenda replied.

"I'm in the middle of a conference call with Mr. Murphy and my mother," Dove replied a little caution.

"Do you mind if I listen in?" Tony more insisted than asked.

Dove frowned at him then turned to Brenda.

"I told him about TAT."

Dove sighed. "Brenda, I asked you not to tell anyone about that."

"That wasn't a wise call," Tony stated. "Introduce me to your mother and ask her to allow me on the call." He took Dove's hand. "I promise I have your best interest at heart."

Brenda nodded. "Just let him listen in and ask a few questions. I think he may be able to help."

Dove hesitated. "Okay." She turned and followed Brenda as she walked towards the kitchen.

Tony whispered, "Belle St. Clair? Really?"

Dove looked over her shoulder at him, surprised. "You didn't know who I was?"

"No, how would I? You didn't say anything."

Her laughter filled the room. "I didn't think I had to. Wow you really know how to bruise a woman's ego." She walked into the kitchen smiling. "Mr. Murphy, could we put you on hold for a minute?" She hit the hold button on the phone.

"What's going on?" Lark asked.

"Mother." Dove smiled up at Tony. "This Anthony Perry. Anthony my mother Lark Warren."

"It's a pleasure to meet you, Mrs. Warren."

"The pleasure is mine." Lark smiled. "Wait until your Aunt Carole puts her eyes on this one."

Tony looked confused.

Dove laughed. "I'll protect you from Aunt Carole."

Brenda laughed aloud. "There is no protection from my mother."

Dove waved the conversation off. "I'll explain later. Mother, I would like for Anthony to listen in on this call. Brenda thinks he may be helpful with the TAT situation."

"Oh, all right. Umm... we'll tell Kenneth he's one of your new reps." She released the hold button. "My apology, Kenneth. Mr. Anthony Perry arrived. He is Dove's new entertainment rep. He has a few questions regarding the TAT situation. I'll turn this portion of the meeting over to him."

Tony took a seat. "Mr. Murphy, Anthony Perry here. I'm going to leave the business details regarding Ms. St. Clair's commitment with KJ Music on the table. The only portion I wish to discuss at this time is her involvement with Trevor Allen Thomas, who performs as TAT. I reviewed the morality clause in her contract and believe we may have an avenue in which to sever any professional ties between Ms. St. Clair and Mr. Thomas."

"I'm all ears, Mr. Perry."

"You have a felon who has been in possession of a firearm."

"His people are claiming the weapon belonged to someone else," KJ explained.

"You're speaking of the night of the incident in the club. I'm referring to multiple times while on tour," Tony declared. "A close examination of your morality clause indicates any illegal activity is cause for re-negotiation or termination of the contract. As this time, Ms. St. Clair wishes to exercise her rights to withdraw from any further legal obligations with Mr. Thomas."

There was silence on the other end. Dove and Lark held their breath until KJ spoke. "My legal team thinks you may have something there, if the violation can be proven. Give us a few days to run down some details. If this pans out, we may be ready to seal this deal."

"We'll look forward to your call, Kenneth." Lark beamed as she disconnected the call.

"This could cut you off from TAT completely," Brenda added.

"For now, I'm just happy to know we found a way to legally break away without KJ Music having to pay a price."

CHAPTER FOURTEEN

"I can't believe I had the answer to this situation and didn't know it," Dove said as her mother stepped out of the room to call her father.

"I can't believe I've been kissing on Belle St. Clair and didn't know it."

They both laughed.

"That's funny. I had no idea you didn't recognize me. Why did you think I was wearing the hats to cover my face?"

He shrugged. "I never questioned it."

"KJ was really impressed with you and Brenda."

"Knowing the criminal side of law comes in handy more times than people may think," Brenda huffed.

"I remember when I told you about TAT carrying a gun, you knew then, that he had broken the law." Dove shook her head. "I had no idea."

Tony didn't respond. Dove turned to look at him. "What's wrong?"

"We need to talk about you and I."

Dove had a feeling this conversation was coming. "All right. I don't feel this is the place."

"We can go to my place. You can cook that dinner you promised and we'll talk there."

Dove stood. "I'll let my mother know we're leaving."

Tony watched as she walked from the room and wondered what he was going to do. At this point he wasn't in so deep he couldn't walk away. But did he want to? That's the question he had to answer. Did he want to walk away from a woman who made his heart sing. Tony walked up the steps and met Dove in the foyer.

"Are you ready?"

"Yes."

Brenda watched them from the landing above. "I hope you two know what you are doing. I can't have your love life interfering in my job promotions."

Tony shook his head. "We're just going to talk."

"Un huh. I've seen the kind of talking y'all eyes been doing." Brenda turned then walked away laughing. "People have been known to end up pregnant from that kind of talking."

"She is getting to be too much like her mother," Lark commented. "Go on, enjoy your evening."

♩♩♩

On the way to his condo, they stopped at the market to pick up a few items for dinner. It may have been his imagination, but to Tony it seemed as if everybody and their mothers recognized Dove the moment they entered. Noticing his discomfort, Dove took his hand as they scanned the aisle for different items she would need to cook. At one point, they stopped in the vegetable section, picking out peppers when Tony bent over and whispered, "I think a man is following us."

Dove continued checking the peppers. She looked up at him, with the brim of her cap shielding her face and had the nerve to smile. "I deal with them all the time." She held up two peppers. "Red or Yellow?"

"Red."

"Spicy." She dropped the pepper in the basket he was holding.

"This doesn't bother you?"

"Frankly, it gets a little old after the first few times." Then she shrugged her shoulders as she picked up an onion. "And then you realize, it's really a compliment. It shows me that I touched someone's life in a positive way with my music. What better tribute is there than that." She put the onion in the basket.

Tony kept an eye on the man as they moved to the broccoli. "I think we should leave."

"I think we should keep shopping," she said. "I need some carrots."

"Why do you go through this?"

"How else am I supposed to get my groceries?"

He looked down at her questioning face. There was a sweetness there that caused him to smile. "This is just a day in the market, isn't it?"

"See, you got it. It's just a day in the market."

With that, he bent down and kissed her lips. "You are something." He took her hand and moved on to the carrots. "This is one of those things we're going to have to talk about. I'm not feeling the strange men following you around the store thing."

"Let's check out." She took the basket and made her way to the cash register.

Tony looked back but the man was nowhere to be found.

Dove gasped as she entered his condo. "What a beautiful view."

"It's the reason I purchased this unit." Tony dropped his keys on the stand next to the entrance then walked into the kitchen. He placed the bags on the breakfast bar that separated the living room from the kitchen then looked up. The vision of Dove standing in front of the floor to ceiling window with the back drop of the sun setting on the river was breathtaking. She removed her cap and the band holding her hair in a ponytail, freeing her gorgeous mane. She then ran her hands through it, separating the strands into a full natural style, ending with a big fluffy cotton ball.

"That feels good," she started saying as she turned towards him. Her words stopped as her eyes settled on him.

It was in that moment he knew the woman standing there was meant for him.

"It looks good." He walked to where she stood in the middle of the floor, he ran his fingers through her hair and marveled at its softness. He pushed her hair back, cupping her face with his hands. Her eyes filled with anticipation, as he took his time memorizing each eyelid as he kissed it, the small pert nose, as he touched it with his, the sweetness of her lips as his tongue slid across them.

"Do you remember those consequences we spoke about the other day?"

Her hands covered his as she gazed into his eyes. "I recall telling you I'm looking for love. What are you offering, Anthony?"

His tongue eased between her lips. The touch of their tongues sent chills down his spine. His arm eased over her shoulder down to her waist, merging their bodies. Her breasts touching his chest, their thighs brushing against each others, all began a melody of Slow Jam that played in his mind. Their tongues moved in rhythm, her arms wrapped around his neck making the kiss deeper, more intense. The air around them became sexually charged; his hand slowly caressed her back, down to her behind, pulling her close to feel his need that was spiking with every twist of their tongues. Lifting her from the floor, her legs wrapped around him causing a moan to escape from his throat. Her lips trailed across his cheek, down to his throat where she proceeded to kiss right under his chin.

"Dove." He sat her on the sofa, pulled the midriff top over her head then burrowed his lips between the rise of her breasts, kissing, then running his tongue across the top as he upheld the front of her bra. Lingering for a moment on the beauty of them, he took one nipple into his mouth and sucked relentlessly. Her head fell back, her legs spread wider allowing him to rest his need deeper in the v between her legs. The heat was so intense he knew the clothing separating their skin would incinerate. His mouth moved to the other nipple, as his hands unzipped her jeans. He lifted her with one arm, the other hand went beneath the back of the jeans, pulling them down her legs. The thong left her skin exposed to his hands and he relished in sucking her nipples as he hands squeezed the smooth skin of her behind. She ripped his shirt, sending buttons flying across the room causing both of them to laugh, but neither willing to lose the skin-to-skin connection. He stripped the jeans and strappy sandals from her feet, dropping them to the floor. His tongue trailed from her breasts, to her navel. He pulled her legs wider, placing her thighs over his shoulders. His finger moved the thin strip of lace to the side and his tongue dove to her middle. Kissing and sucking as she squirmed under the assault of his mouth on her. His tongue dipped in and out, determined to put his mark on what he now considered his. Her moans and the feel of her nails on his back pushed his need to bring her full circle. He wanted to feel her release, see the look in her eyes as she rode it out. His thumb brushed against her clitoris, as his hand squeezed her behind and his mouth sucked until he could feel her lips contracting, her body tense and the scream escape. Lifting his head, his lips captured hers for a deep soul stealing kiss. Then he sat back on his haunches. His hands massaging her thighs as he watched her body jerk from the orgasm wrecking through her.

It was the most exquisite vision he had ever seen. Her breasts rising and falling, her hips moving upward, her eyes watching him watching her.

He stood, removed his pants, dropping them to the floor. His need erect, long and hard, protruding from his body, jerking as his eyes took in the sight of her remarkable body ripe and ready to take him in.

"I'm offering forever. Are you ready for that?"

The lids from her eyes were nearly closed, her lips swollen from the passion filled kiss, the juice from her release on her legs. He wanted to be inside of her, but not before he heard from her.

"Yes," she whispered. "I'm ready."

He positioned his body on top of hers, wrapping his arm around her waist, lifting her hips until his need touched her entrance. Her tightness sucked him in. The heat surrounded him like the warmth of being home. He pushed deeper as his body covered hers. Her legs locked around his waist, taking him deeper into the depth of her love. There were birds singing, in his ears. He swore it was, but it was Dove singing in his ear, "This is love, this is love, deep inside of me, like this is just love."

Her voice, husky and sensual, spurred his senses, causing him to dive deeper and deeper reaching for the pinnacle of the love she was offering. Her words turned to a moan, as her nails dug into him, then to a scream when they both exploded with the release of their lovemaking.

The two lay there holding each other. Their breathing was in tune with each other's, hands lovingly caressing.

Dove had never felt anything so beautiful in her life. Oh, she had sex before. Now she knew that was all it was, sex. This was what it felt like to be loved. Tony adjusted his body moving her to rest on his chest.

"TAT is gay." She let that hang in the air. It wasn't clear why, but she wanted Tony to know the truth about her relationship with TAT. "We were a cover-up for his fans. I inadvertently walked in on him and one of his boys when we were on tour. He begged me not to say anything and I agreed. I really didn't see anything wrong with it. You love who you love." She was circling her finger around his chest. "I think these people he signed with know and are using that to blackmail him. Or he could be afraid I will go public."

"First, let me say I'm not unhappy to hear about his sexual preferences." He kissed her forehead. "However, people are dangerous when their backs are up against the wall." Tony sighed. "The best thing for him is to come clean. No one can hold it over his head."

Dove shook her head. "He can't. Have you ever listened to his music? If it came out that he was gay, it could ruin his street cred. At least that's what he thinks."

"He's living a lie and that comes with complications. Do you believe he will follow through on his threats?"

Dove hesitated. "I've never seen him do anything, but his boys do talk about his tantrums. It sounds as if he follows through on his threats."

Tony tightened his arms around her. "He's not going to be happy when he receives the request to dissolve your agreement. I think Mr. Murphy was right to get you away from him, for now."

Dove could feel the tension in his body. He was concerned about her safety. That was the last thing she wanted on their first night together. She positioned her body over his, lying on his chest with her chin resting on her hands. Her eyes captured his. He put his hands behind his head, giving her a better view. She liked the way his eyes twinkled when he looked at her.

"I'm in deep, deep like with you. Does that scare you?" She watched his lips form into a smile.

"I was in deep, deep like before we came into my home. Now, I'm at the beginning of love. Does that frighten you?"

She couldn't hold back the smile. "To the contrary, it thrills me. My career deals with a lot of fake people. I want and need, real love in my life. Someone who loves me, Dove, and can handle Belle."

"I haven't experienced Belle...Yet."

"Well..." She slid down his chest, leaving a trail of kisses along the way. "Belle is the wild child." She kissed his navel. "You never know what she may do." Before he could react, she had captured him in her mouth, causing him to raise up off the sofa almost bucking her to the floor. He reached out and caught her shoulders, just as she tilted.

"Oh my lord," was all he managed to get out before she took him completely over the edge.

CHAPTER FIFTEEN

The next few days were heaven for Tony and Dove. He would go to the office and she would stay at his place working on music. TAT's representatives received KJ called indicating the documents for dissolution. He sent the new contracts, and once her mother and Tony reviewed it, she signed them and celebrated her new beginnings. By Saturday, Tony felt it was time for her to meet his family. He knew his mother would be thrilled he finally had a woman in his life. What he did not count on was his niece Jasmine's reaction to meeting Dove.

"Mom," Tony called out from the living room.

"I'm in the kitchen," Elaine yelled back.

"Hey," he said as he released Dove's hand and kissed his mother's cheek.

"Well hi, yourself," she said as she wiped her hands on her apron. "Who is this?" Elaine smiled.

Tony reached out his hand. "This is Dove Warren." He put his hand around her waist. "Dove, this is my mother, Elaine Perry."

"It's nice to meet you, Mrs. Perry. Tony has told me so much about you."

Elaine took her by the hand and led her to the table. "Well he hasn't told me anything about you. In fact, I haven't had more than a good morning and good night from him all week." She laughed. "Now I know why."

"Mom," Tony warned.

"Oh hush up and pour us a cup of tea." Dove smiled up at Tony. "So tell me about yourself."

Jasmine walked into the kitchen with her earplugs in her ear, dancing and singing to a song she was listening to.

"Hey, Uncle Tony," she said and continued singing.

Tony recognized the song and started singing and dancing with her. Jasmine unplugged the earplugs from the phone and placed it on the counter with the music playing through the speaker. Dove stood behind Jasmine and started singing and dancing to her hit song Driven.

Jasmine turned, dancing and screamed right in Dove's face. She started jumping up and down pointing. "Oh my god, oh my god, it's Belle, Uncle Tony, it's Belle."

Tony and Elaine were laughing. He put his hands on Jasmine's shoulders to stop her from moving.

She clamped her hand over her mouth to stop screaming.

"Dove, this is my screaming niece, Jasmine."

Dove took Jasmine's hand, then slowly embraced her. As if it was the most natural thing to do. "Hello, Jasmine, you like Driven?"

"Yes," Jasmine suddenly seemed like the sixteen-year-old she truly was.

"You know I do so many ballads it was great to finally have a song I could move to." The whole time she talked to Jasmine she was calming her down by talking about music, dancing, engaging her in other topics like her classes. It was amazing to watch her operate.

Elaine walked over to her son. "Who is she?"

"She's going to be your daughter-in-law one day." He walked over and joined the ladies at the table.

Later in the afternoon, his sister Karen and her boys joined them. After the initial shock of seeing Belle St. Clair in their grandmother's house, everyone settled down and Dove fit right in. To Tony, this was what family was all about.

♩♩♩

"Boss." Pete walked into Fazi's office. "You have company from Atlanta."

Fazi looked up. "Lou." He extended his hand. "I didn't expect a visit?"

"This situation called for a personal touch," Lou explained. "This is TAT, he's the client."

Fazi extended his hand. "TAT."

"Yeah, man. So, where's Belle?"

There is this thing called respect Fazi believed in. He was old school. You get a feel for the people you work with. Trust was a big issue in his business. If his gut didn't trust you, he proceeded with caution. His gut didn't trust this man.

"We have a man on her." Fazi pulled his hand back, then glanced at Lou. "Why don't we take a seat."

"I didn't fly down here to sit around." TAT looked at Lou. "Time is money. I got people waiting on me."

"Fazi is the best at this," Lou explained. "Let's take a minute to talk through our next step."

Pete glanced at Fazi. "You want me to get a location, Boss?"

"No," Fazi replied as he glared at TAT. "Ray has his check in time. We can wait."

"I need to handle this and head back to Atlanta."

"What exactly do you need to handle?" Fazi asked.

"My business," TAT replied.

"When you're in my town, using my people, it becomes my business."

Lou intervened. "We need her signature on a contract. Once we get that, we're out." He placed an envelope on the desk. "Here's our payment."

Fazi opened the envelope, then fanned through the bills inside. "That's a healthy sum for a signature?" Fazi questioned. "Does your man here have something else in mind?"

"That's not my concern," Lou explained. "My job is to get her to sign this contract, by any means necessary. He's here to help me convince her to do just that."

"Just a signature?" Fazi questioned.

"Yeah," TAT echoed, "Just a signature."

Fazi wasn't nobody's fool. Lou may be after a signature, but that TAT guy, no, he wanted something else. He could see it in his eyes.

"Pete here is going to take you to the location."

"We just need the address," TAT said. "We don't need him to come along."

"As a courtesy, I insist." Fazi's demand was clear.

"We appreciate that Fazi," Lou stood motioning for TAT to do the same.

Fazi stood. "Pete will meet you at the car." He waited until Lou and TAT were out of the room. "My gut don't trust that guy. Wear your earpiece. I want to know what's being said every minute."

"You got it, Boss."

♩♩♩

"We been sitting here for over an hour," TAT complained. "Where in the hell is she?"

Pete, making small talk with Lou who sat in the passenger seat, looked back at TAT who was sitting behind Lou. "This is a part of the job. We chill until she gets here."

"I ain't got all night to take this chick out. I need this done and get my ass out of here."

"We're here to get a contract signed," Pete reminded him then turned back to Lou. "Am I wrong or is something else going down here?"

"He's the client," Lou stated. "His dime."

Pete glared at Lou. "You putting your rep with the Boss in jeopardy for this client?"

"No. I'm here to get a signature. What he does is on him."

Pete's phone buzzed indicating a message was coming through. "Location" was all it read. Pete sent the message back to Fazi.

Fifteen minutes later the back door to the SUV opened. Fazi slid in. "Evening, gentlemen."

Lou nodded. "Didn't think you came on these jobs anymore?"

"Only when my gut indicates I need to be on the scene."

"I'm the client. You got your payment. Your presence isn't needed and neither is your man."

"My town." Fazi glanced at TAT just as a vehicle passed them.

"That's them, Boss," Pete announced. "We can follow them to his place from here."

"We can take her right here," TAT said.

"His place is more isolated and less chances of being seen," Pete suggested.

"You don't even know if she's leaving with him."

"He has been tapping that all week." Pete laughed. "I don't see that changing."

Everyone inside the SUV adjusted. They watched as the vehicle made a u-turn at the corner then parked in front of the house. A man stepped out of the driver side of the vehicle. He walked around the vehicle and opened the passenger door.

Fazi recognized him, but couldn't place a name. Something told him to proceed cautiously. "Call our man at Richmond PD. Give him the license plate number. I know this guy."

"I don't want the guy." I want her." TAT made a move to get out of the vehicle.

"Nobody moves until I get a reading," Fazi demanded.

"The plate came back to an Anthony..."

Before Pete finished, Fazi said, "Perry...he's an attorney."

"Our guy says he's the DA for the city of Richmond."

They continued to watch as the woman stepped out.

"That's Belle," TAT hissed with excitement.

Fazi put his arm out holding TAT back. "No one mentioned a DA. I'm not bringing that kind of heat on my organization." He sat forward. "We have a rule. We don't do law enforcement or their family. This Perry guy falls into that category as far as I'm concerned."

"I don't want him," TAT yelled. "I want her taken out. I don't even know who he is."

"Looks like he's her man." Pete shrugged.

"Which puts us right back where we started," Fazi stated. "We don't do law enforcement or their family."

TAT pushed the door open. "The hell with that."

CHAPTER SIXTEEN

"I so enjoyed meeting your family." Dove smiled as she stepped out of the car into Tony's arms. "I could hang with them every weekend."

"They loved you, too." He kissed her lips, as she wrapped her arms around his waist. He turned their bodies and began walking her backwards up the sidewalk that led to Brenda's front door. "You get your clothes." He kissed her neck. "We're going back to my place." He kissed the other side of her neck as she giggled. "I'm going to show you a few tricks." He picked her up in the air.

Dove's arms went around his neck as he kissed the crease between her breasts.

"TAT."

Tony sat her down. "I'm kissing you and you're calling his name?"

She hit him on the chest and point across the street. "No, TAT."

Tony turned to see a man standing behind an SUV pointing a gun in their direction.

Tony wrapped his body around Dove's knocking her to the ground, shielding her from the bullets that rang out. Pain, like fire, ripped through his shoulder causing him to cry out.

Fazi opened fire through the window on TAT, dropping him to the ground. He jumped out, slammed his fist on the top of the SUV and yelled, "Get Lou out of here."

Dove pushed Tony's body off of her then screamed. "Tony." Her hands frantically ran over him to find where he had been shot.

"Let me check him," a man said from behind her. He reached over and checked Tony's pulse. "He's alive." He slapped his face. "Perry, Perry, open your eyes."

Tony's eyelids slowly opened. Dove cupped his face as she cried. "Tony."

Fazi looked into Tony's eyes. "This is your one." He then disappeared.

Brenda opened the door, saw the commotion, then ran to Dove. "Get up, get up." She pulled at her.

"No, no, Tony's been shot." Brenda leaned down. "His back," Dove cried out. "Help me turn him over."

Brenda did as she yelled to her neighbor, "Call the police. Tell them the DA has been shot." She then tore her blouse, to apply pressure to the wound.

Within minutes the block was loaded with police, emergency vehicles, and detectives. An officer yelled, "There's a body over here."

Officers ran in that direction. "We got a weapon."

"Check for active shooters in the area," a commanding officer shouted. "We got a DA down, full alert."

The EMTs arrived and began working on Tony. Just as they loaded him into the ambulance, television crews began to arrive. Before the area was roped off, one of the cameramen got a shot of the body across the street.

"Holy crap. That's TAT, the rapper."

♩♩♩

The next twenty-four hours was a media frenzy as the death of TAT filled the airways. Reporters were scrambling for details as KJ Music's public relations team kicked into gear.

Elaine and Karen were at the hospital when Tony came out of surgery. Dove, Brenda, Lark, and Martin, were there as well. They all waited there, supporting Dove as she relayed, the best she could, to the police what happened.

"Did you see anyone else?" a detective asked.

"The man who checked Tony to make sure he was alright."

"Man?" the detective asked. "What man?"

"I don't know, a neighbor or somebody," Dove explained. "I was checking Tony, I wasn't paying attention to anything else."

"Ms. Warren." The detective sounded irritated. "You did not have a weapon and neither did DA Perry. Who shot TAT?"

"It's clear she doesn't have an answer to that question, Detective." Brenda stepped in. "She has indicated twice, she did not see the man. Now, if you don't mind, I think that's enough questions for now."

"I do mind," the detective replied.

"Then I suggest you mind somewhere else. She isn't answering any more of your questions."

"You're an ADA, I would think you would understand how this goes. There is an active shooter somewhere out there."

"Then go out there to look for him." She pushed Dove towards the family, effectively blocking the detective from her cousin.

Hours later, Tony's eyes fluttered open. He didn't feel much of anything except dry lips. His tongue touched them. The moisture felt good.

Then there was something cold. Ice... it registered with him. Yes, ice. It felt good on his lips. He turned to the angel that relieved that discomfort and smiled.

"Dove."

She kissed his lips, he closed his eyes and retreated to the blackness.

The next time he awakened to Dove on the side of his bed, his mother was in a chair on the other side and an officer was sitting in a chair near the door.

"Certainly is a lot of folks in this room," said a female in a white coat with an electronic tablet in her hand. "Good morning, Mr. Perry. How are you feeling?"

"Tractor trailer on my chest."

"To be expected." She smiled. "You look good for a man who just took a bullet for his woman. I have to say you brought some excitement around this place."

"Happy to oblige."

"I have a couple of detectives that are insisting on speaking with you. Are you up to it?"

Tony tried to sit up, then flinched from the pain. "Let me do that." She reached over adjusting the bed. "I'll let the detectives in."

The action caused Dove to wake up.

"Tony."

"Morning." He attempted a smile. "Wasn't quite the night I had planned. What happened?"

"We prefer she not answer that until we speak. How are you, DA Perry," Detective Grimes asked.

"John, what's homicide doing here?"

The detective looked around at the people in the room. "You don't know?" He continued when Tony gave him a negative shake of his head. "Trevor Allen Thomas, better known as TAT the rapper, was killed right across the street from where you were shot."

Tony frowned then began to remember. He took Dove's hand. "Are you okay?"

She squeezed his hand. "I'm fine, thanks to you."

He nodded then looked back up at the detective. "He was across the street. There was a black SUV, he was behind it. I saw him raise a gun and point it towards us. I covered Dove and we fell to the ground. I don't know what happened after that."

"Did you fire back?"

"No. My weapon is in my car."

"You didn't see anyone else with Thomas?"

Tony thought, then shook his head. "No."

"Are you back at it again, Detective," Brenda said from the doorway. "There is a decent timeframe when a man is shot before you should question him, you know."

"I have a case to solve, Ms. ADA. You interrupt with me again and I'm going to arrest your fine, dimple ass. Do I make myself clear?"

Tony tried to laugh at Brenda's expression, but the pain was a bit much.

"That's enough for now." Elaine stood. "Unless you plan on arresting my old ass, I think it's time for you to leave. You can come back and ask your questions later."

The detective looked from Elaine to Brenda to Dove then shook his head. "You got some mean, fine women protecting you. I guess I can pull my men off. But I have one more question. We pulled the license plates of the vehicles some of the neighbors' cameras caught in the area. Will you take a look at these?" He placed four pictures on the bed. "Do you recognize any of these men?"

Tony looked at the pictures. The second one from the left caught his attention. He knew the man. It was Mr. Defazio, Susan's father. He remembered the man thanking him and saying he owed him one. Then he remembered the man's face standing over him saying. *That's your one.*

He shook his head. "I can't say that I do."

The detective nodded. "Okay, that's all for now. You get better. We need you to keep your ADAs in order." He winked at Brenda as he left the room.

Tony and Dove stared at Brenda. "What? I didn't do anything to him."

"Looks like he has plans to do you," Elaine said as she bent over to kiss her son's cheek. "You caused my heart some trouble last night, son. Try not to do that again."

"Won't happen again, Mom. Go home. Get some rest."

Elaine nodded. "I'll be back later to check on you. Dove, the doctors will take care of him. You get some rest."

"Yes, ma'am, I will."

"Everyone is getting out to get some rest," the doctor said. "I need my patient to sleep for a while."

She looked at Dove. "You have one minute to get you some sugar, then you are out of here," she warned with a smile then followed everyone out the door.

Dove held his hand as she leaned over the bed. "I am so sorry this happened to you." The tears were forming in her eyes. "I would have never put you in that kind of danger." The tear dropped onto his cheek.

He wiped the tear from her cheek. "It's my job to protect my woman." He smiled, closed his eyes and slept.

Dove kissed his cheek, then walked out of the room.

Lark was sitting in a chair outside of the door waiting for Dove.

"Mother, have you been here all night?"

"Of course. Somebody shot at my baby, where else would I be?" She stood and hugged her daughter. The two held on to each other for a long time. Dove allowing the tears to fall while her mother's love eased the fear that had consumed her through the night.

"I could have lost him, Mother. I just found love and just like that I almost lost him."

"I know, baby." Lark held her tighter. "Your grandmother used to say, 'Life is a song worth signing. You have to sing it loud and clear, 'cause you don't know when it's going to be your last song'."

She held her at arms' length. "I think your song with Tony is just beginning." They turned and started walking arm in arm down the corridor. "And I think it's going to be a string of number one hits." She nodded. "Yes, I think it's time to give you the box."

"What box?"

"The one your grandfather made for me. Your grandmother's Timex watch and my keepsakes are inside. Now it's your time to control the box. Then one day you will pass it on to your daughter."

"How do you know I'm going to have a daughter?"

Lark turned to her daughter and laughed. "The way you and Tony looks at each other," she huffed as she her arm around Dove's shoulder, "you will probably have twin girls before the year is out."

The two laughed as they walked out to face the world of the media, together.

Epilogue

One year later Dove read over the invitation again. It was inconceivable that this would happen at this time in history.

"This is something you always said you wanted," KJ spoke. "I've known three generations of St. Clair songbirds. The dream of doing this performance came up every time." He looked at her. "You are the first to have the opportunity to fulfill the dream."

"I realize that," Dove acknowledged. "But does it have to be for this president?"

The people at the table laughed.

"I can certainly understand your hesitation," her father commented. "It would be difficult for me to imagine your grandmother singing for this man."

"She would," Lark commented. "She would sing and keep on singing until love poured from his heart."

"Well, look at it this way." Brenda sat forward. "Your president is asking you to serve."

"He's not my president," Dove declared, then raised her fist in solidarity with everyone else in the room.

"Forever 44," they all chanted.

"Mr. Murphy, how would this impact public relations with KJ Music?" Dove asked.

"There is going to be impact either way. That part of the country who supports this president will boo you, declare you unpatriotic if you refuse. The other part of the country will declare you a traitor to human rights if you do." KJ shook his head. "I hesitated to bring the request to you siting scheduling conflicts. But, I know the personal importance of this request and knew it had to be your decision."

"What do you think, Tony?"

Tony laughed as he shook his head. "This is a family issue. This decision should be made between you all."

Dove gave him an evil eye. "Then you should ask me to marry you so you can help with this decision."

People in the room gasped then grew silent as all eyes fell on Tony.

"Will you marry me, Dove?"

"Yes." She smiled. "Now tell me what to do."

The people in the room laughed and cheered.

"Your grandmother told you music is best when sung from the heart. Can you imagine yourself singing from the heart for this president? The answer to that should be your answer to the invitation."

Dove smiled, then took her mother's hand. "There will be other presidents, Mother. Do you think Grandmother will understand?"

Lark squeezed her daughter's hand. "I think Sparrow is smiling down from heaven at this moment."

"I think so to," Dove nodded. "I'm just as certain Grandmother is having a conversation right now with God about who the next president should be."

'There are always multiple ways to fulfill a dream." KJ sat up. "I think you should go into the studio and record the National Anthem. The recording could be played at events all over the world."

"You can dedicate the recording to your grandmother," Tony added.

"I think that's a wonderful idea." Dove beamed as she sat up. "Mother, you should record it with me."

Lark looked to KJ. "Isn't there a way to blend Mother's voice into the recording? We have her singing the national anthem on tape."

"Hot damn." Martin hit the table. "The St. Clair Belles together again."

"It's possible." KJ frowned. "But, we're not calling them by that name."

"I say give them the proper name and call it a day," Tony suggested.

"What would that be, babe?" Dove asked.

"Songbirds."

♩♩♩

Four years later, the Songbirds' rendition of the national anthem went double platinum for sales around the world. As wonderful as that felt, nothing compared to the thrill of standing in front of millions of people who lined the National Mall in Washington, DC on a crisp sunny day on January 20th. Her parents and now husband, Tony sitting in front smiling up at her.

All the dignitaries had been seated as Dove stepped up to the microphone. She looked to the heavens and said, "This is for you, Grandmother Sparrow." The crowd was silent as her heart filled with pride, and her voice sang out the words to the National Anthem for newly elected President Michelle Obama.

Audiobook available on
audible
an amazon company
THE PENDLETON RULE
IRIS BOLLING
DVDs available on irisbolling.net
Remember, all things flow through...
THE HEART
TELEVISION SERIES SEASON TWO
THE HEART SERIES
BROOKS' FAMILY VALUES SERIES
Fatal Mistake
Teach Me
THE NIGHT OF SEDUCTION SERIES
THE GEMS & GENTS' SERIES
Books available on amazon.com

READ YOU LATER

LA SHEERA LEE

WE READ YOU

BLOGTALKRADIO.COM/READYOULATER

Social Media Strategist

Moderator

Event Planner

READYOULATER.BIZ

Eclectic Palette
Art For
Everyone
eclecticpalette.judithwansley.com

Made in the USA
Lexington, KY
24 July 2017